ZRJC

AUG - - 2022

Peach and Plum

Here We Come!

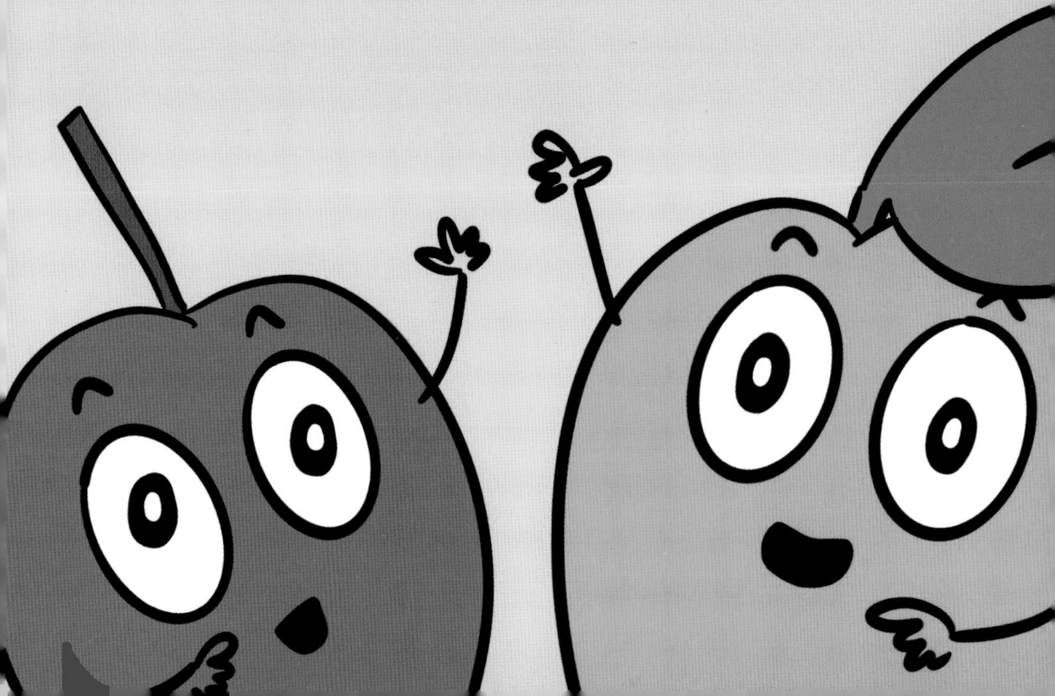

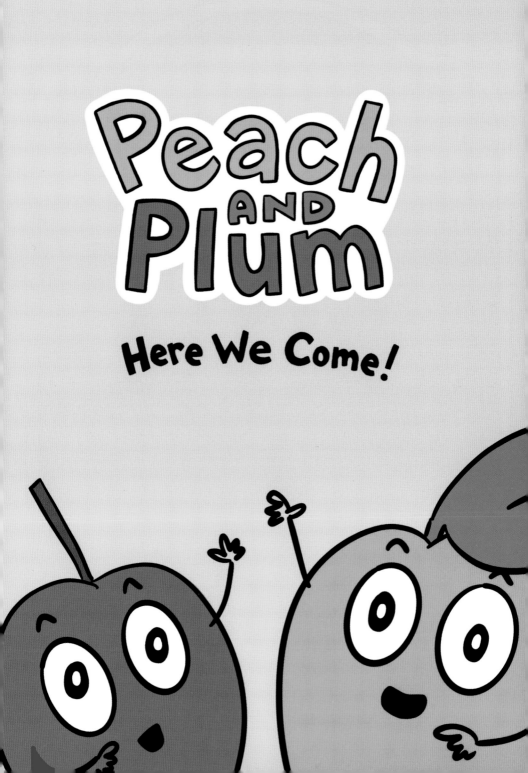

For Trudi

About This Book

This book was edited by Rachel Poloski and Esther Cajahuaringa,
and designed by Carolyn Bull. The production was supervised by Bernadette Flinn,
and the production editor was Marisa Finkelstein.

Little, Brown and Company
Hachette Book Group
1290 Avenue of the Americas, New York, NY 10104
Visit us at LBYR.com

First Edition: August 2022

Little, Brown and Company is a division of Hachette Book Group, Inc.
The Little, Brown name and logo are trademarks of Hachette Book Group, Inc.

The publisher is not responsible for websites (or their content) that are not owned by the publisher.

Library of Congress Cataloging-in-Publication Data
Names: McCanna, Tim, author, illustrator.
Title: Peach and Plum, here we come!: a graphic novel in rhyme / by Tim McCanna.
Description: First edition. | New York : Little, Brown and Company, 2022.
Series: Peach and Plum; 1 | Audience: Ages 6–9.
Summary: In Fruitdale, best friends Peach and Plum enjoy many fun summer activities,
such as playing ball, going to the beach, and riding a bike—although Plum often seems
to find the downside of fun. Told in rhyming text.
Identifiers: LCCN 2021038961 | ISBN 9780316306102 (hardcover) | ISBN 9780316306201 (paperback)
ISBN 9780316344180 (ebook) | ISBN 9780316347242 (ebook other)
Subjects: LCSH: Friendship—Comic books, strips, etc. | Friendship—Juvenile fiction.
Play—Comic books, strips, etc. | Play—Juvenile fiction. | Stories in rhyme. | Graphic novels.
CYAC: Graphic novels. | Stories in rhyme. | Summer—Fiction. | Friendship—Fiction. | Peach—Fiction.
Plum—Fiction. | Fruit—Fiction. | LCGFT: Graphic novels. | Stories in rhyme.
Classification: LCC PZ7.7.M41264 Pe 2022 | DDC 741.5/973—dc23
LC record available at https://lccn.loc.gov/2021038961
ISBNs: 978-0-316-30610-2 (hardcover), 978-0-316-30620-1 (paperback), 978-0-316-34418-0 (ebook),
978-0-316-34691-7 (ebook), 978-0-316-34713-6 (ebook)

PRINTED IN CHINA

Hardcover: 10 9 8 7 6 5 4 3 2 1
Paperback: 10 9 8 7 6 5 4 3 2 1

Peach and Plum

Here We Come!

Tim McCanna

LB
LITTLE, BROWN AND COMPANY
New York Boston

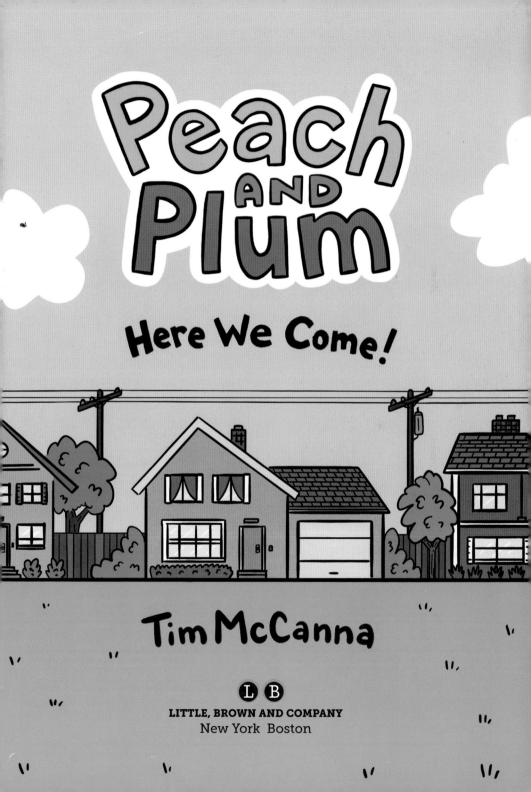

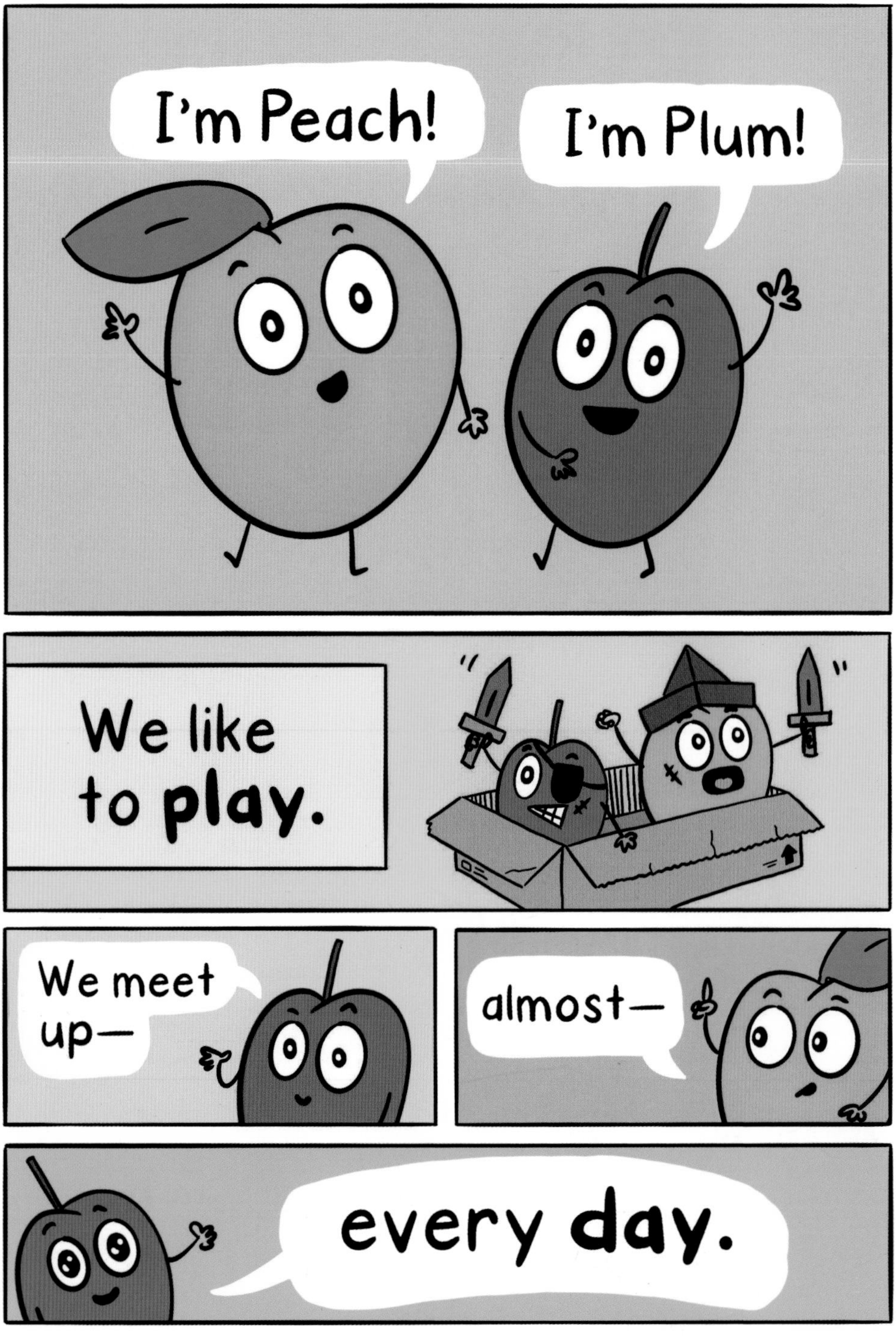
I'm Peach!
I'm Plum!
We like to play.
We meet up—
almost—
every day.

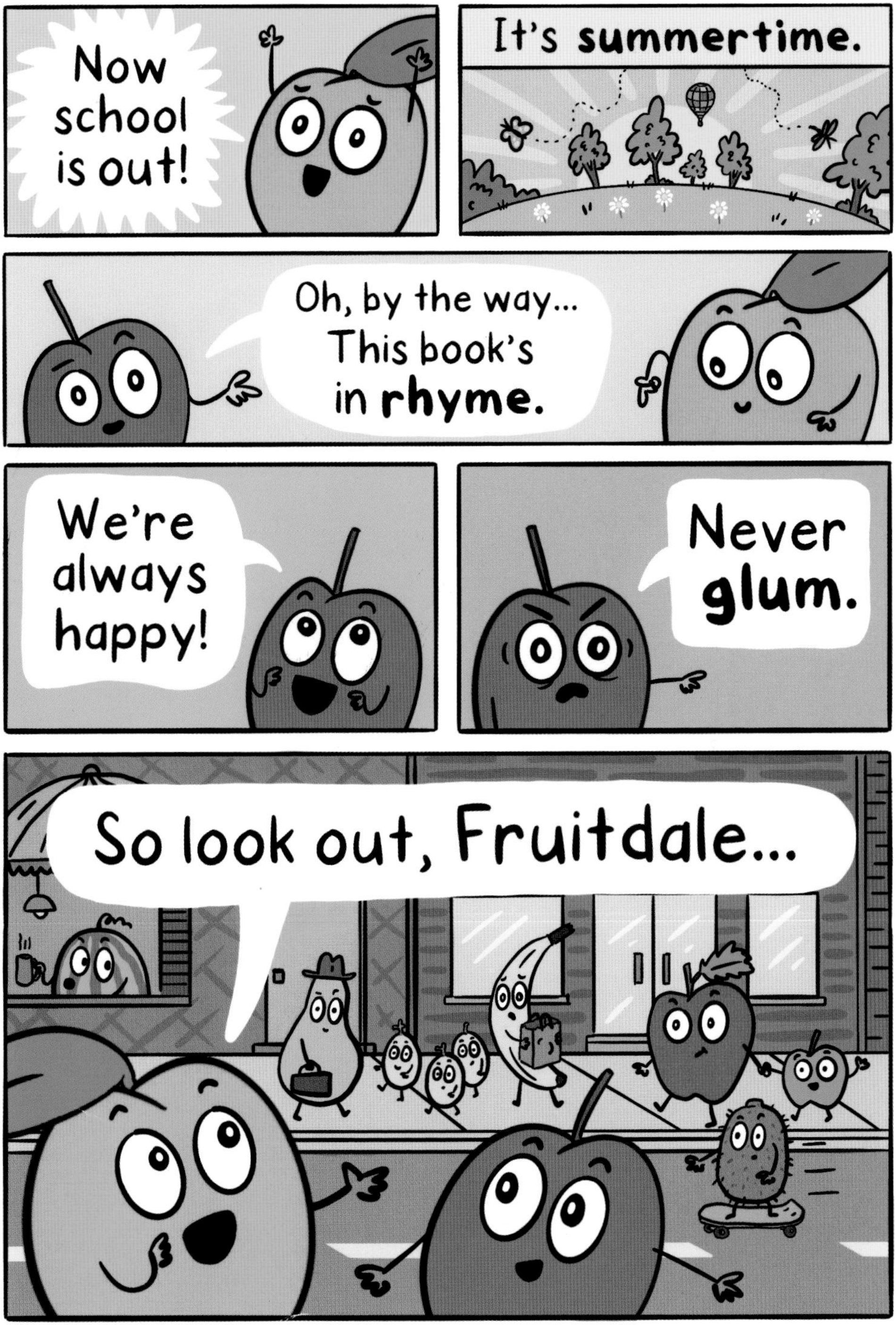
Now school is out!
It's **summertime.**
Oh, by the way... This book's in **rhyme.**
We're always happy!
Never **glum.**
So look out, Fruitdale...

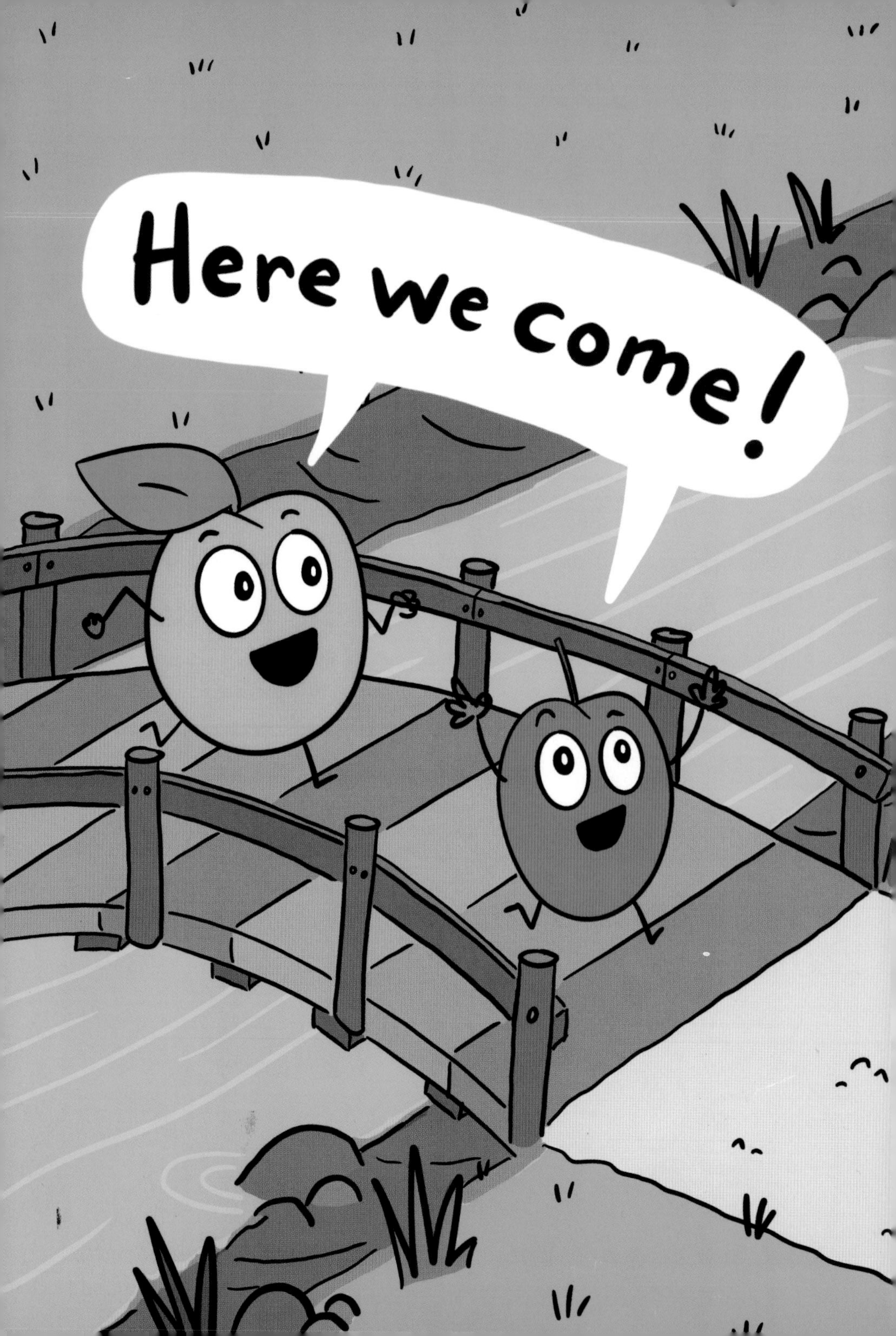
Here we come!

CONTENTS

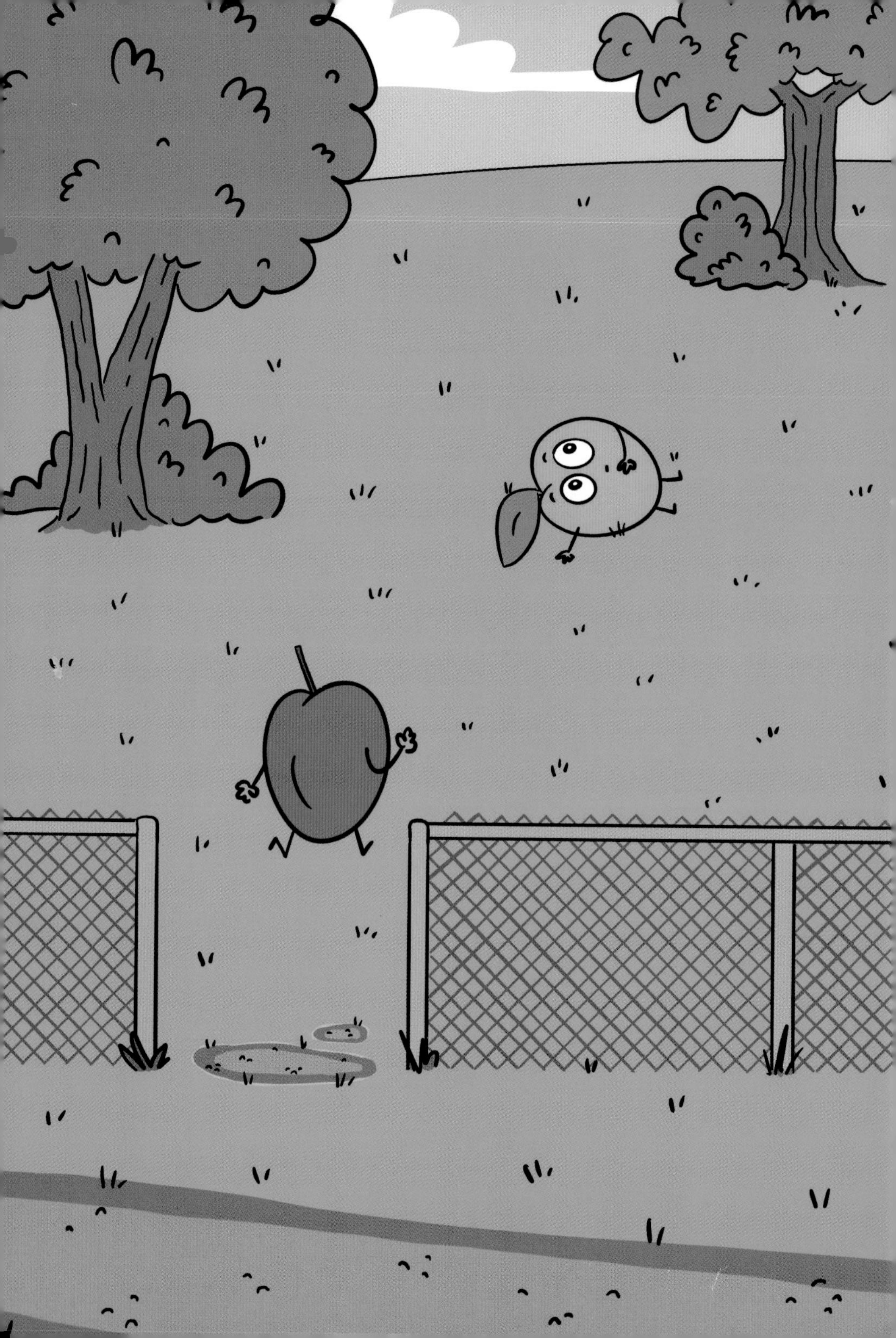

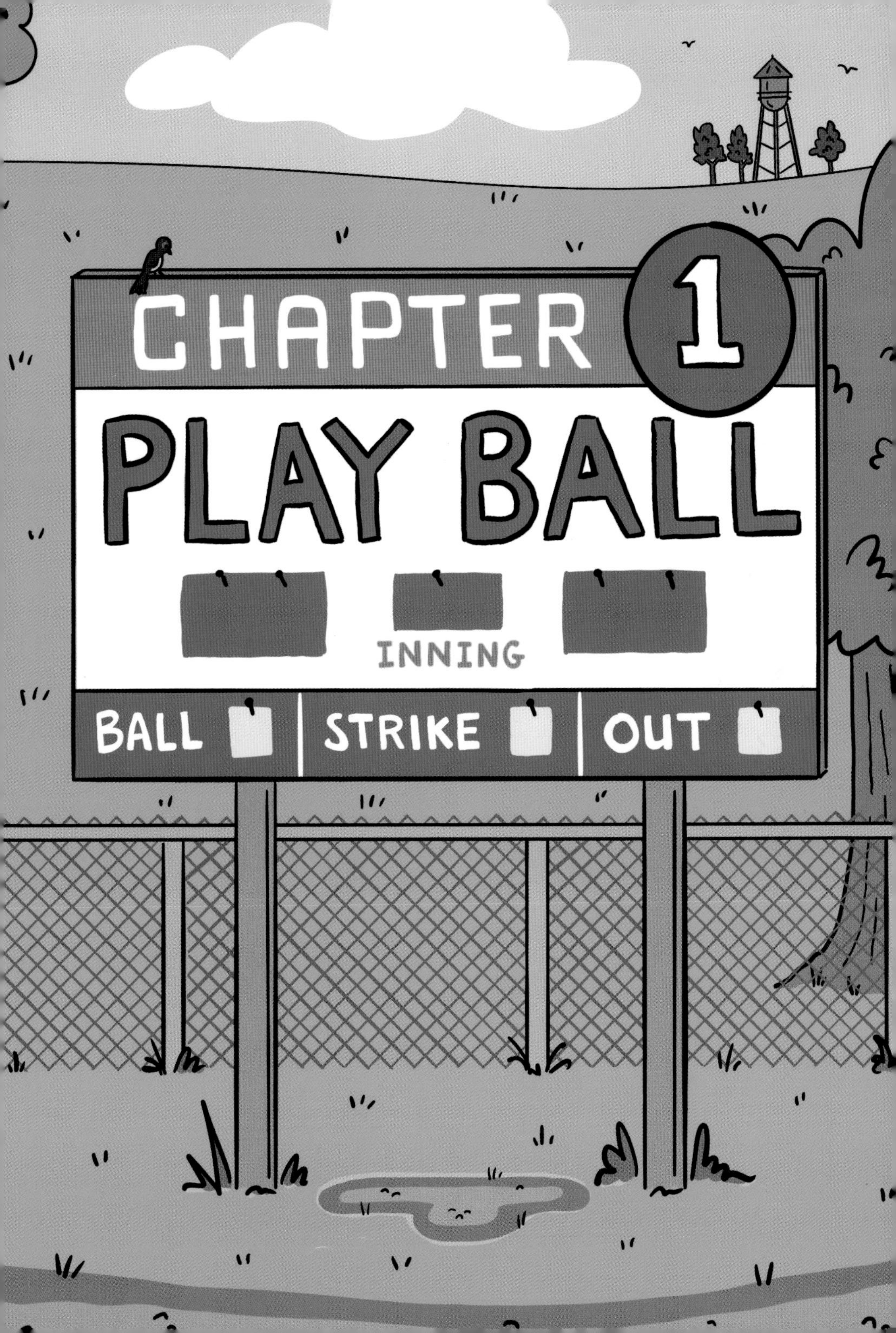
CHAPTER 1
PLAY BALL
INNING
BALL
STRIKE
OUT

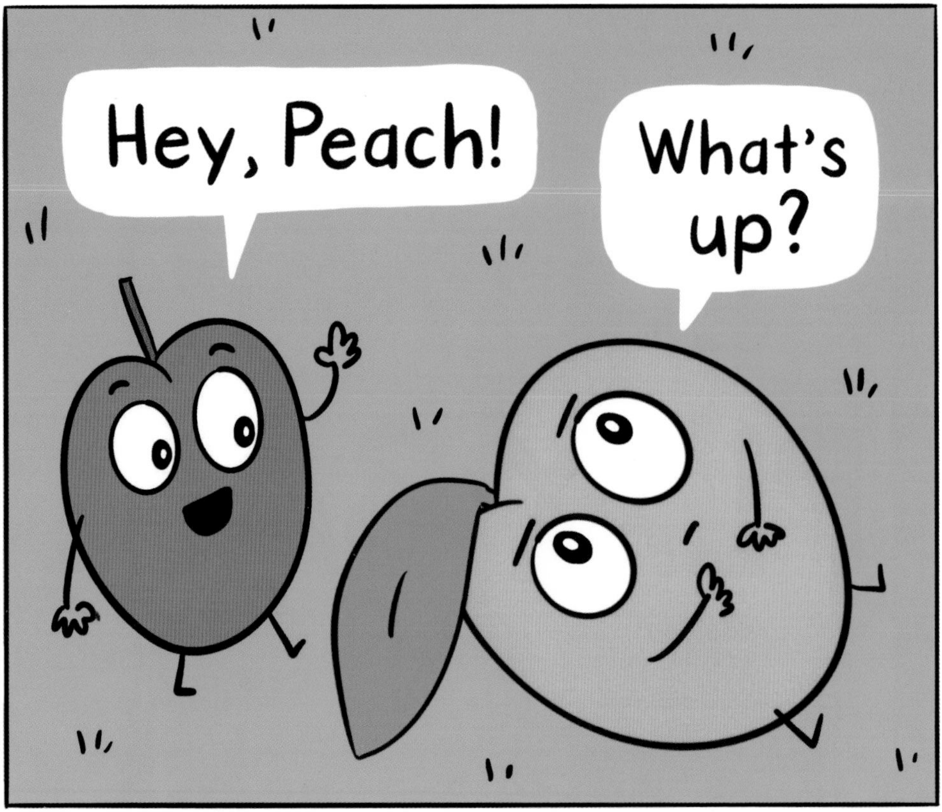
Hey, Peach!
What's up?
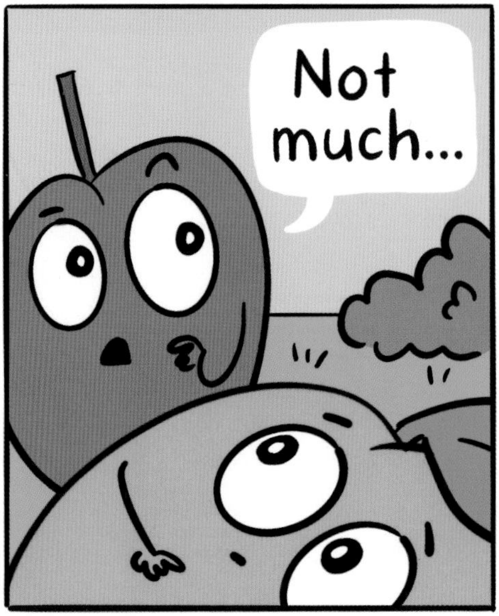
Not much...
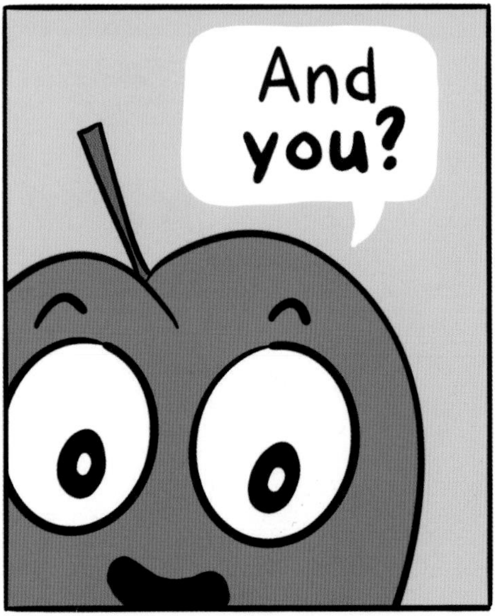
And you?

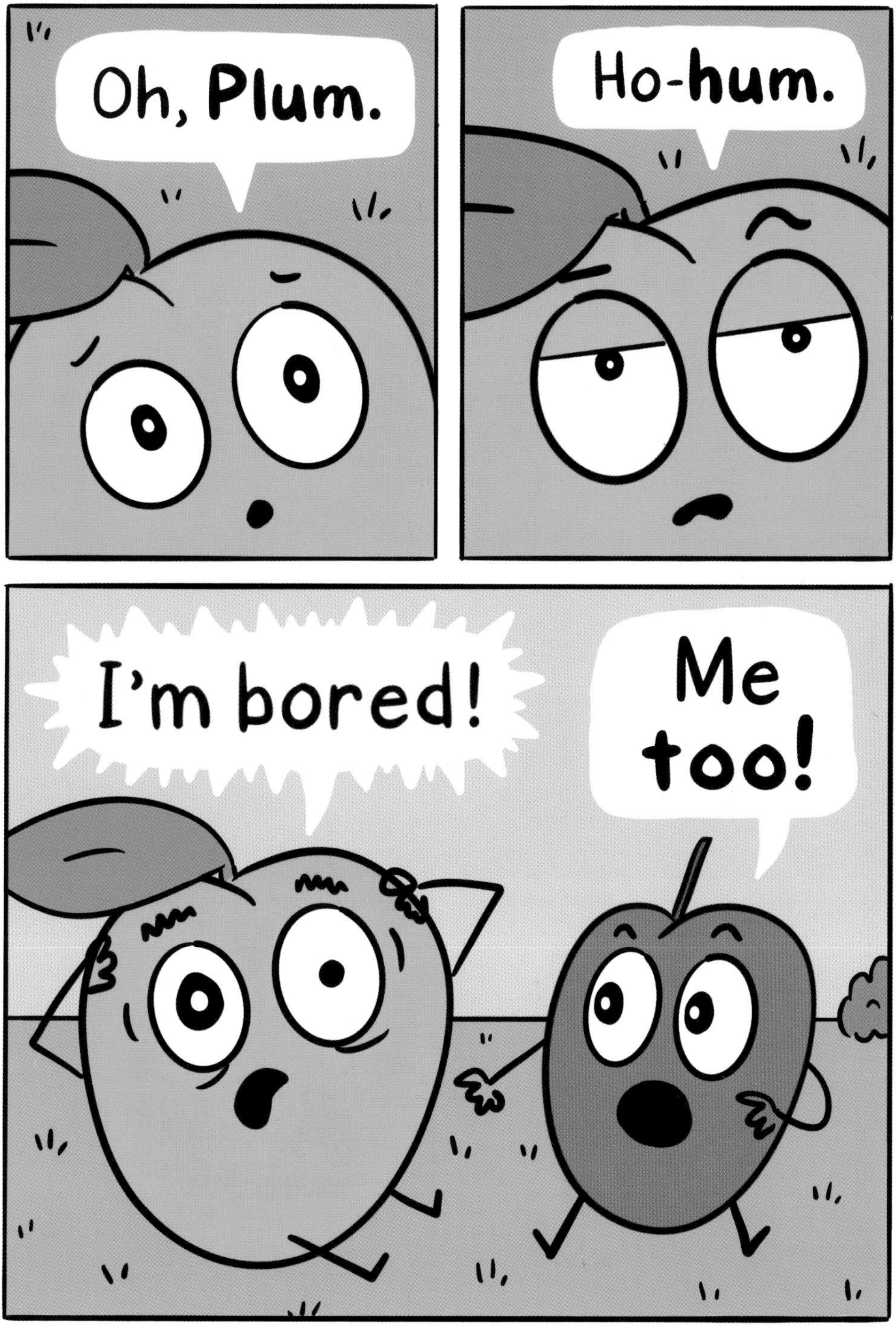
Oh, Plum.
Ho-hum.
I'm bored!
Me too!

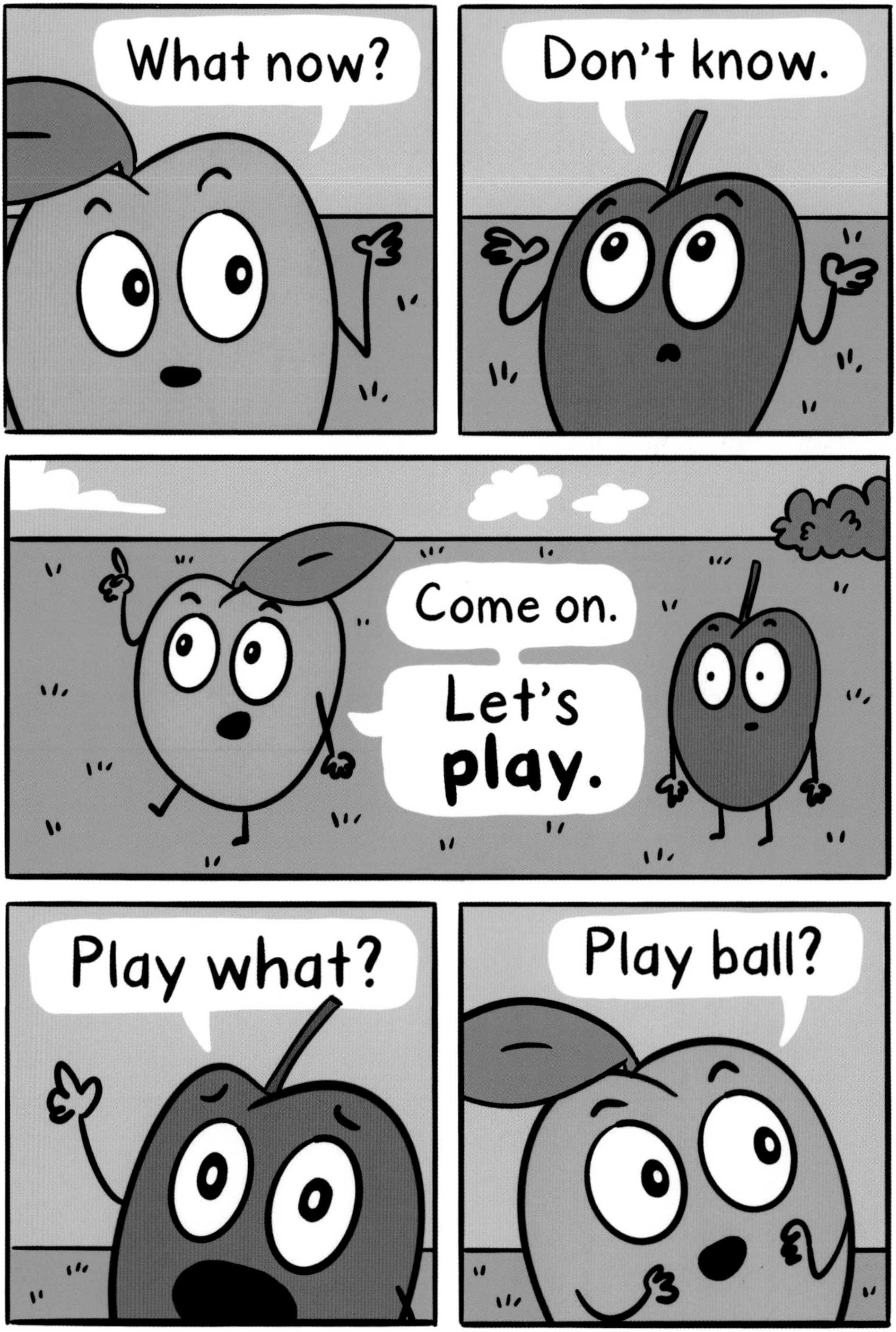
What now?
Don't know.
Come on.
Let's **play.**
Play what?
Play ball?

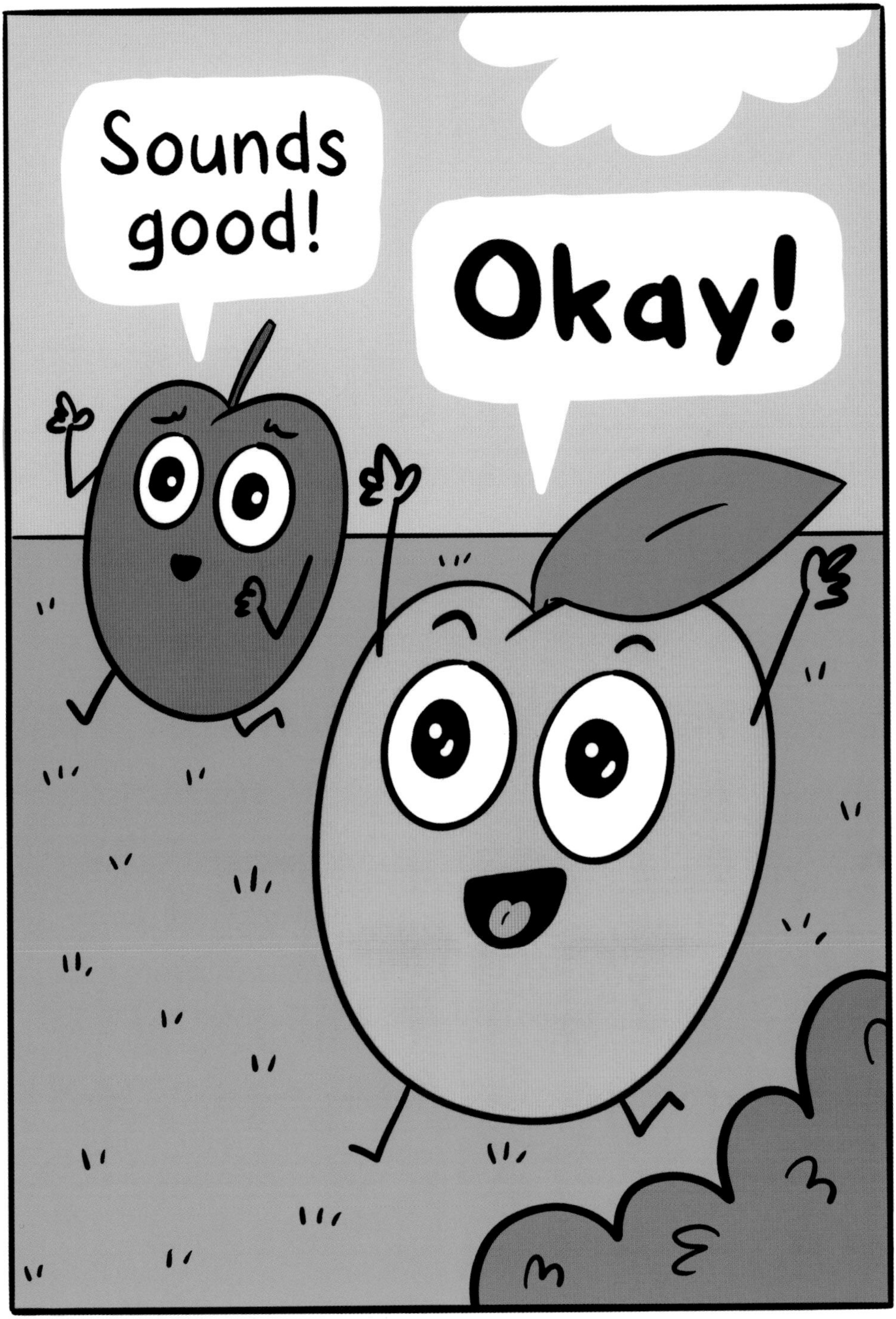
Sounds good!
Okay!

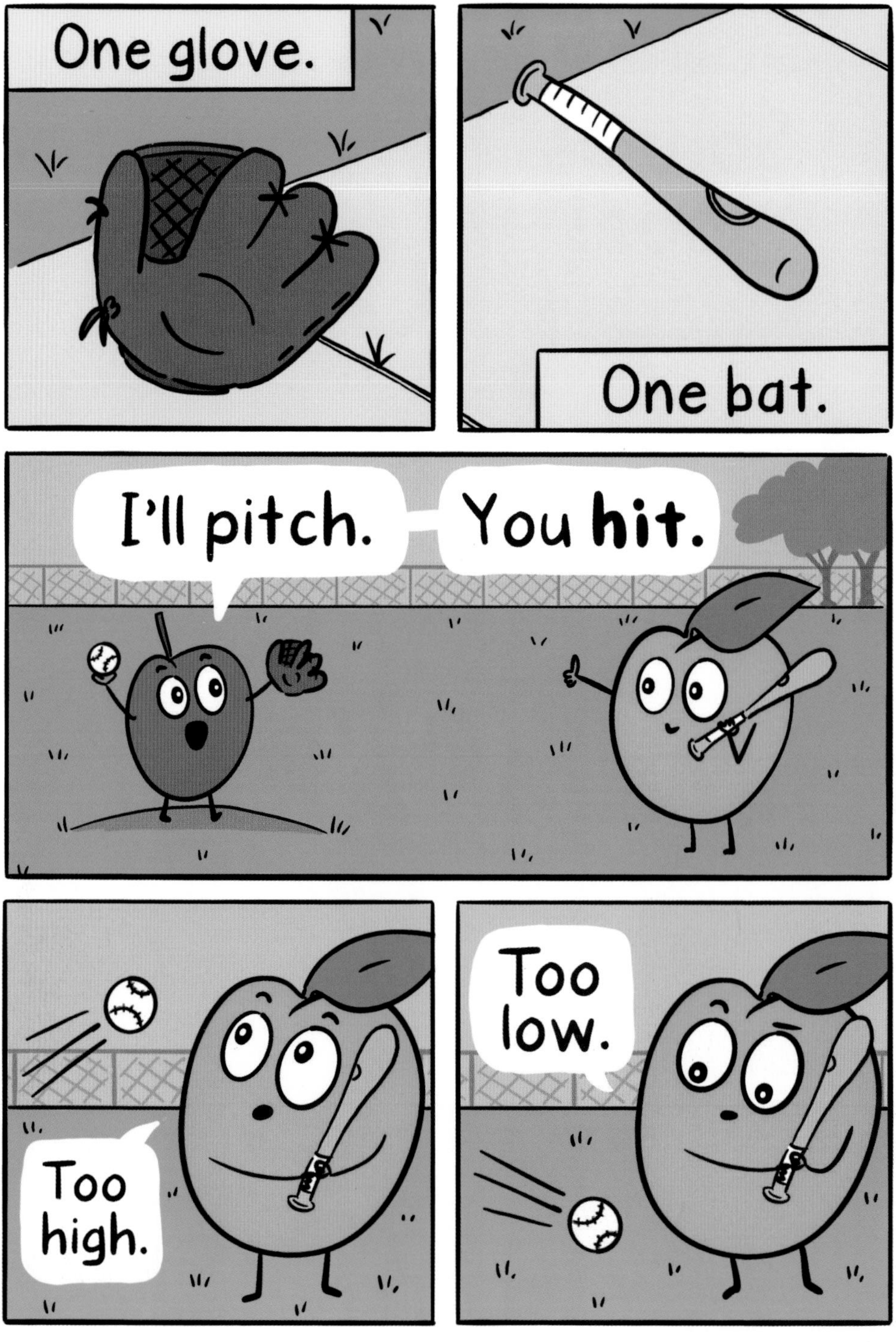
One glove.
One bat.
I'll pitch.
You **hit**.
Too high.
Too low.

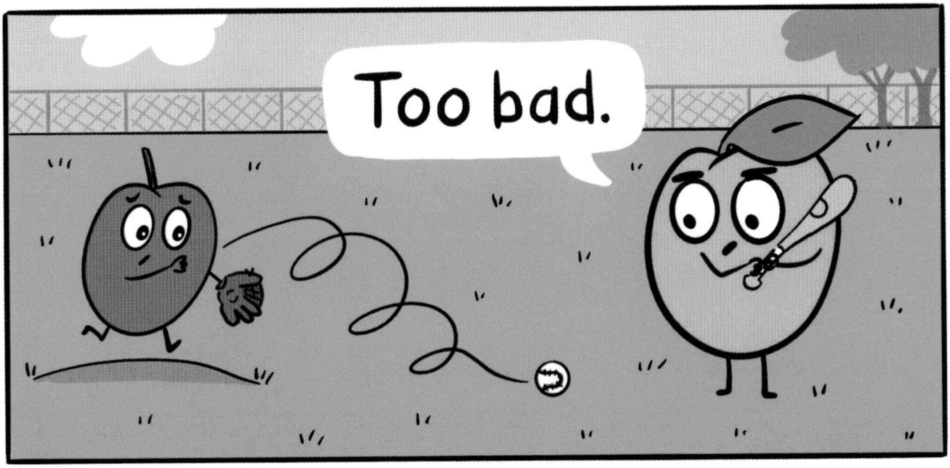
Too bad.

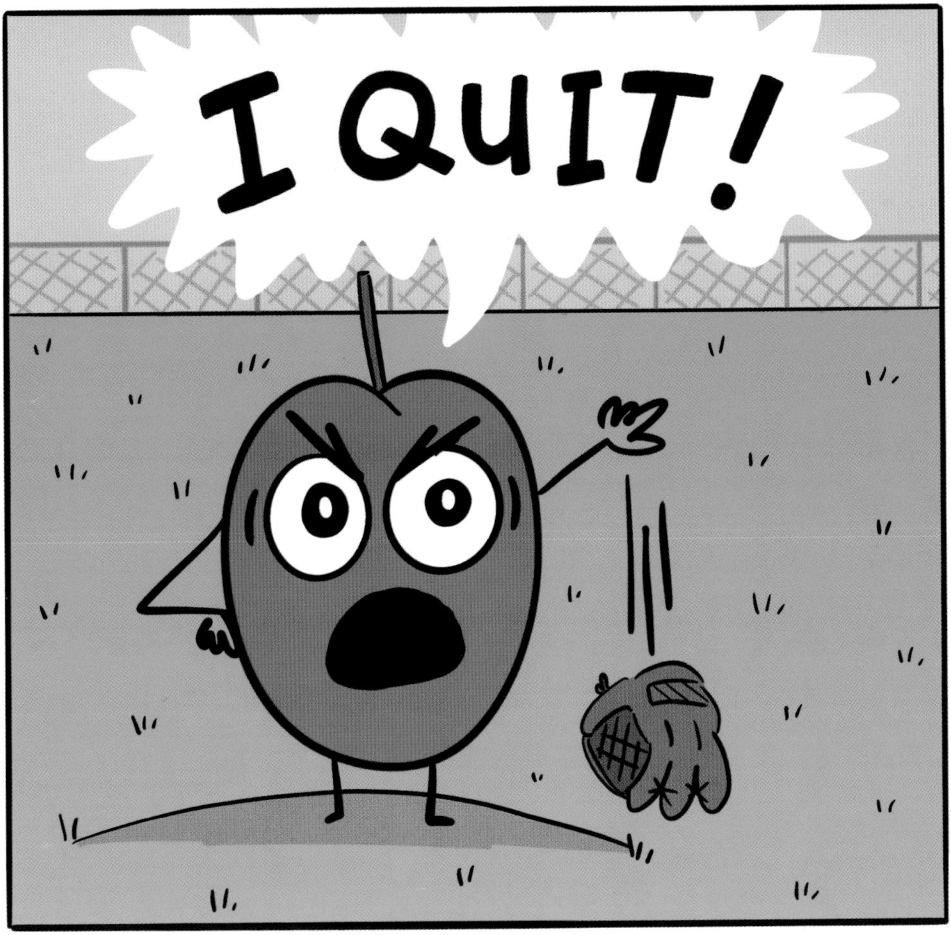
I QUIT!

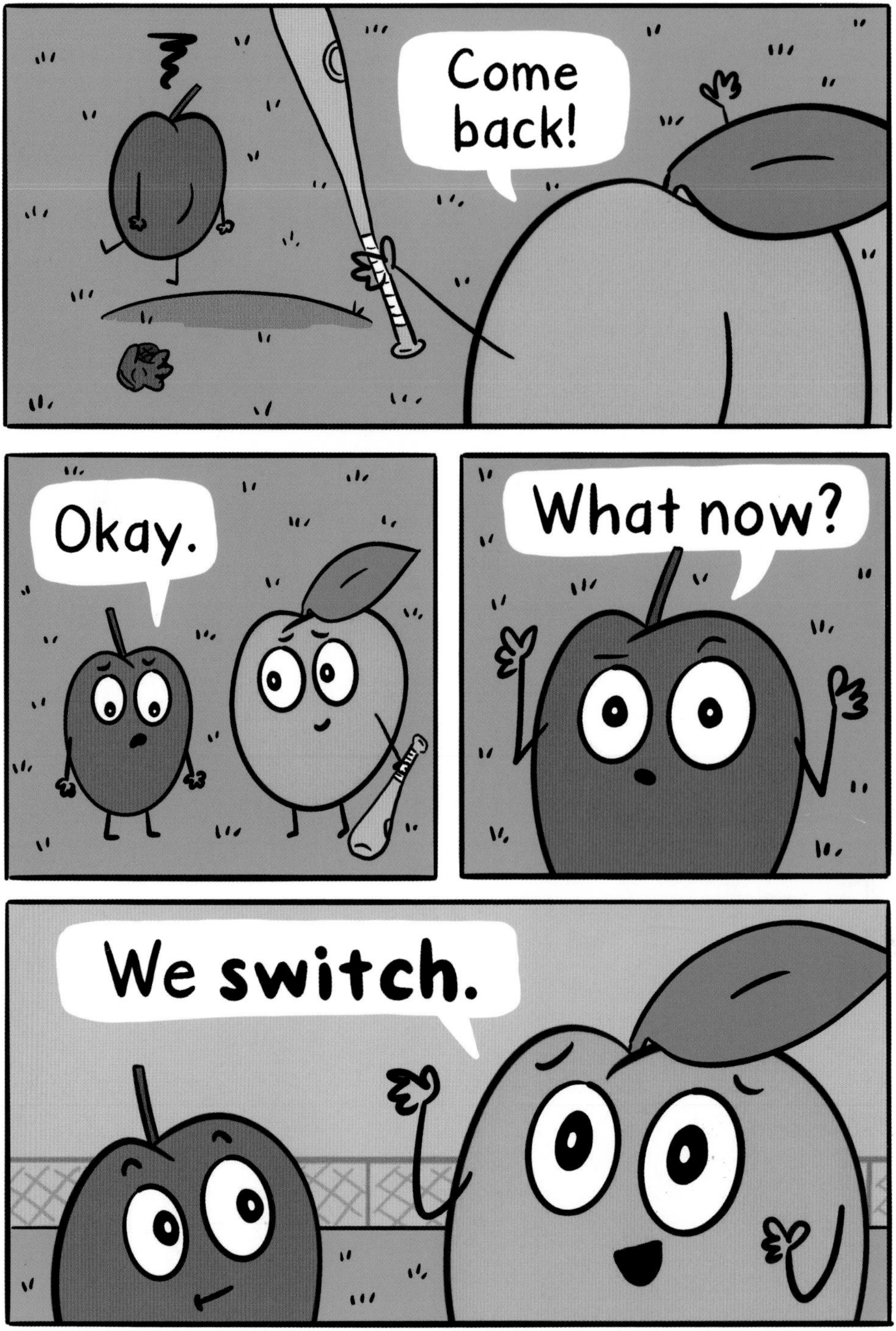
Come back!
Okay.
What now?
We switch.

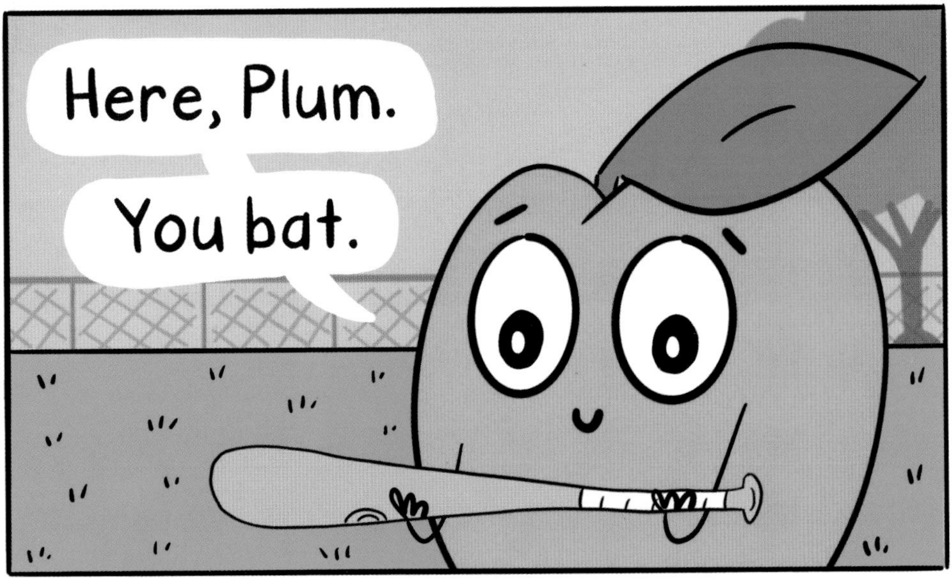
Here, Plum.
You bat.

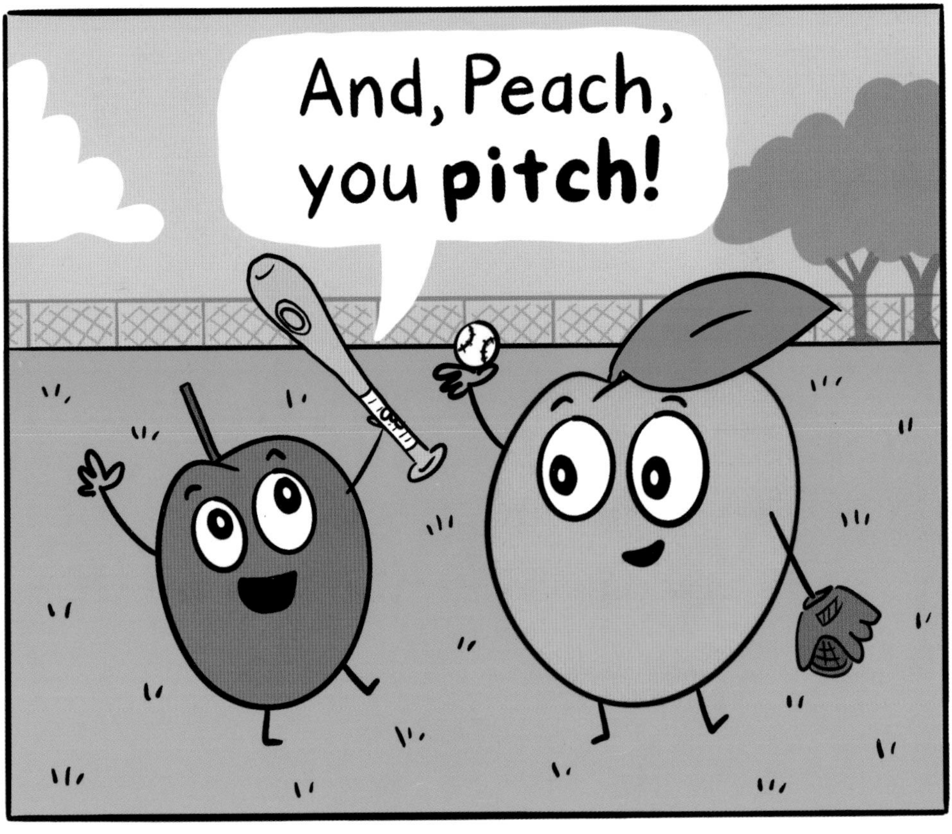
And, Peach, you **pitch!**

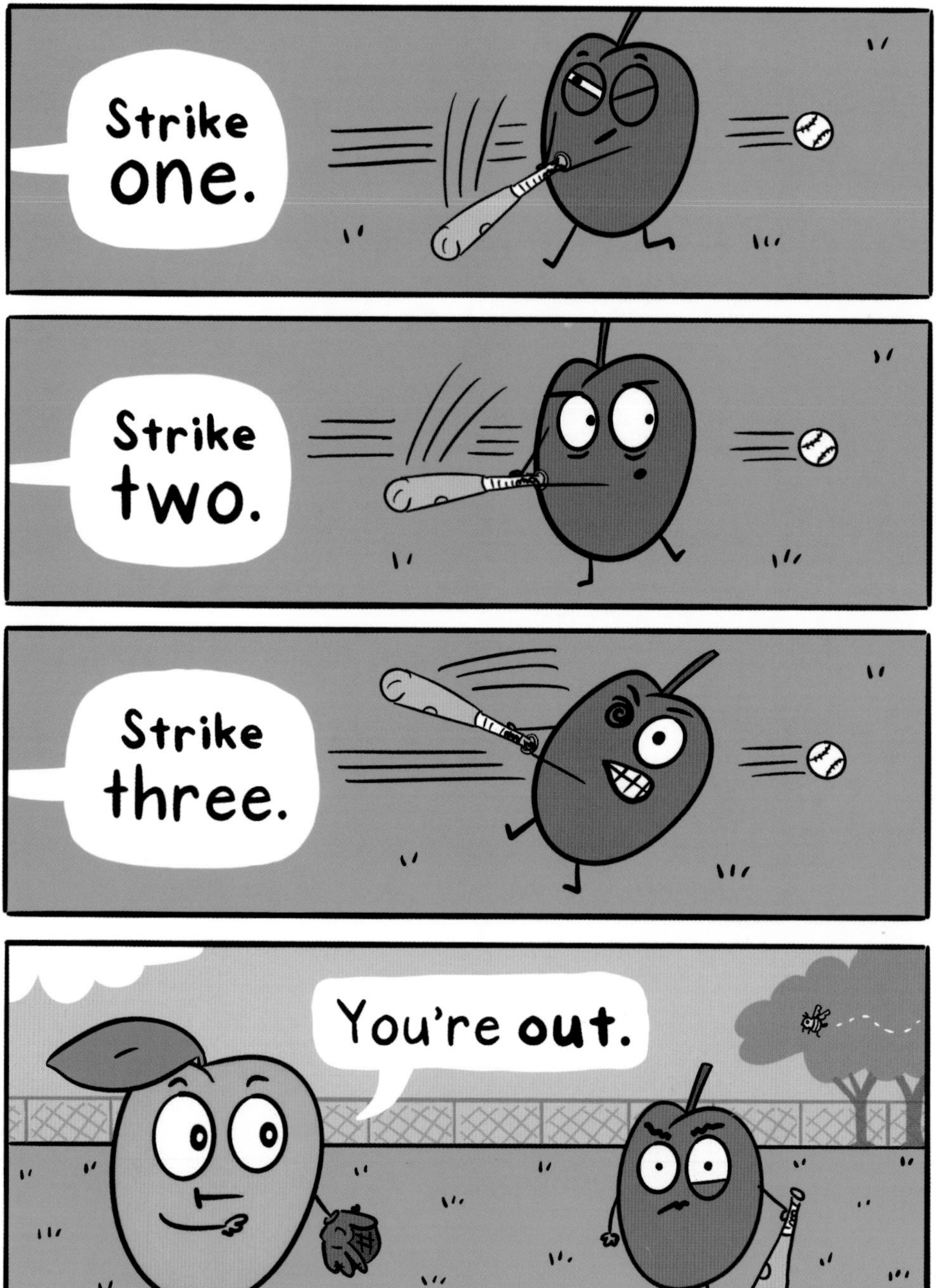
Strike one.
Strike two.
Strike three.
You're **out**.

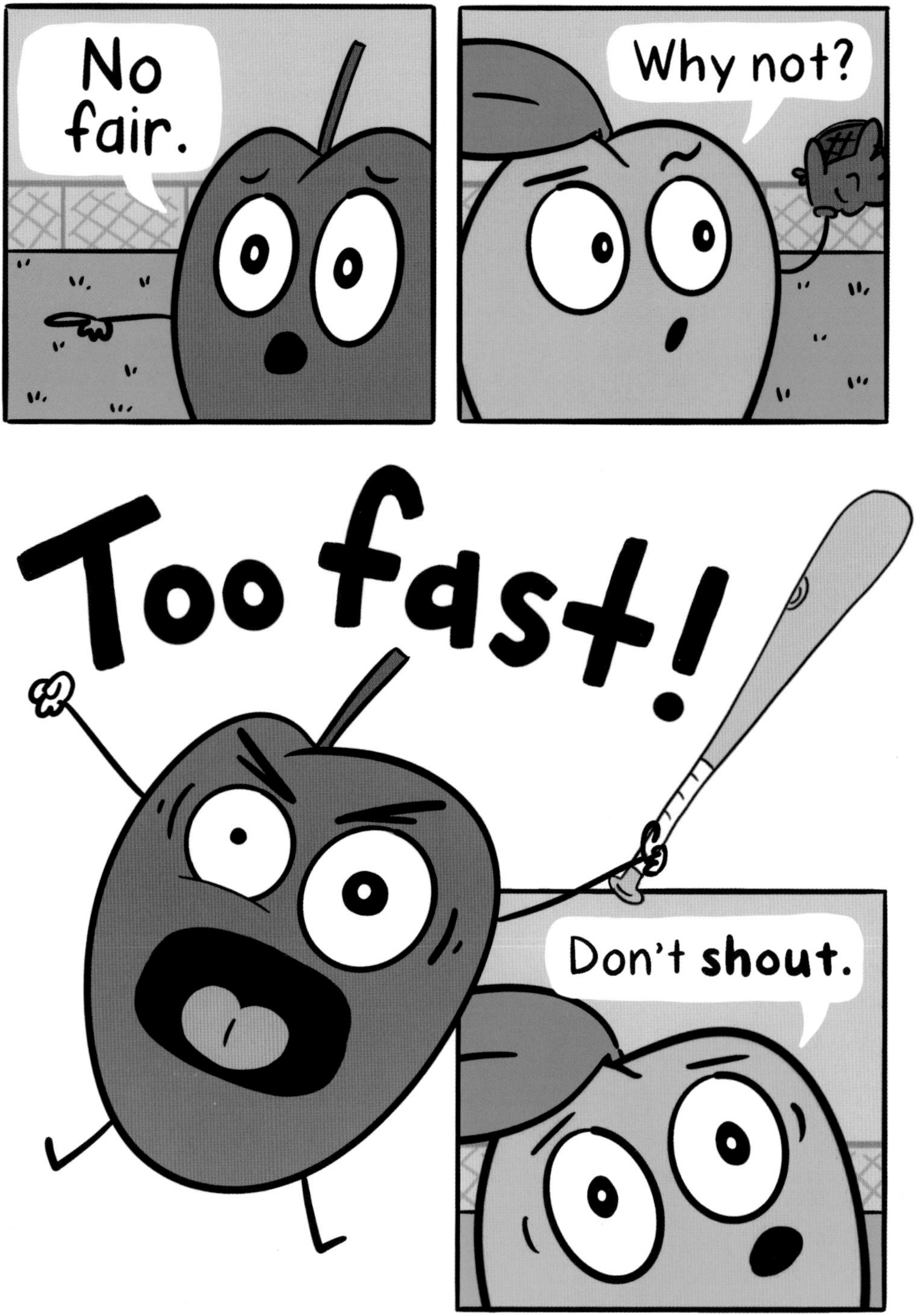
No fair.
Why not?
Too fast!
Don't **shout**.

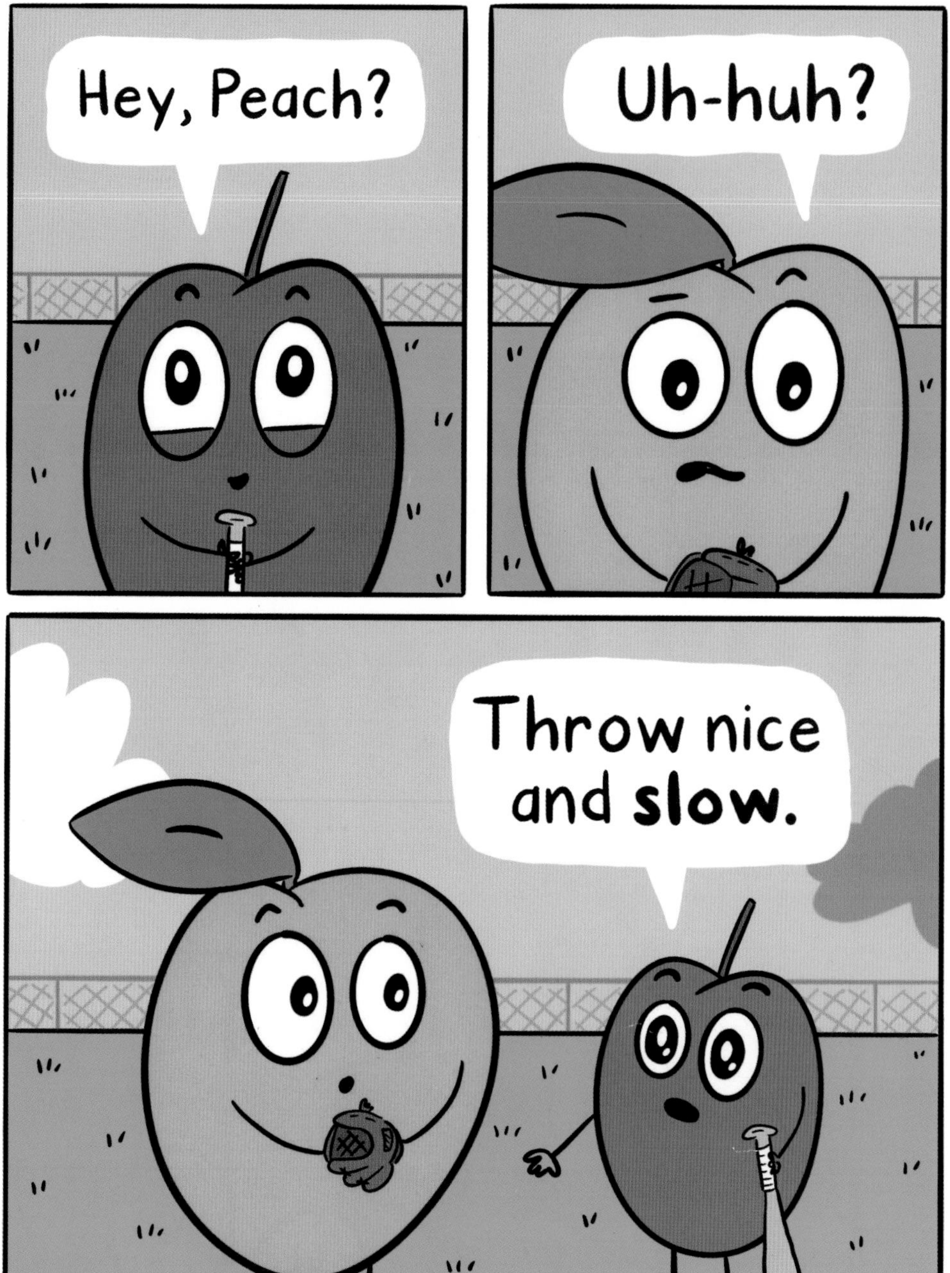
Hey, Peach?
Uh-huh?
Throw nice and **slow**.

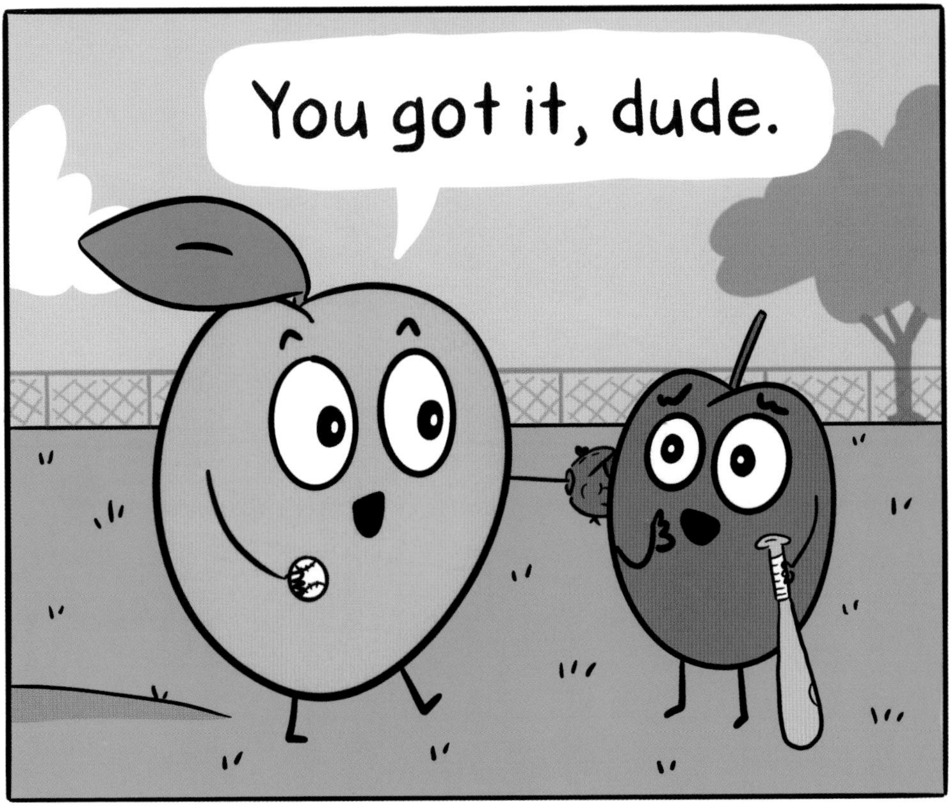
You got it, dude.

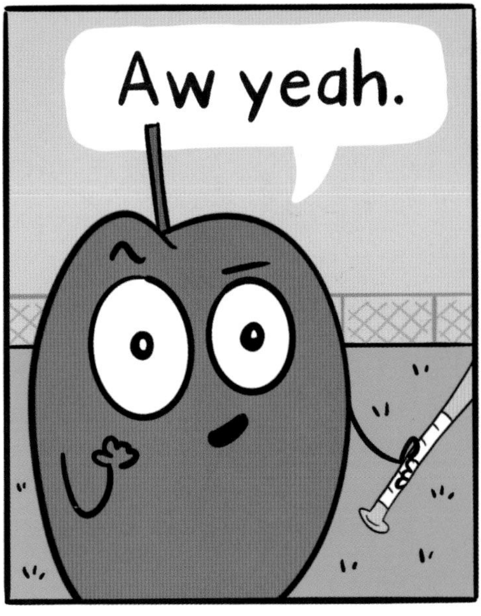
Aw yeah.

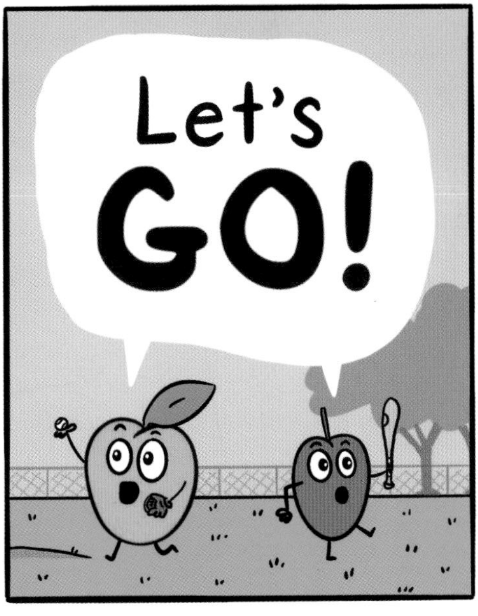
Let's
GO!

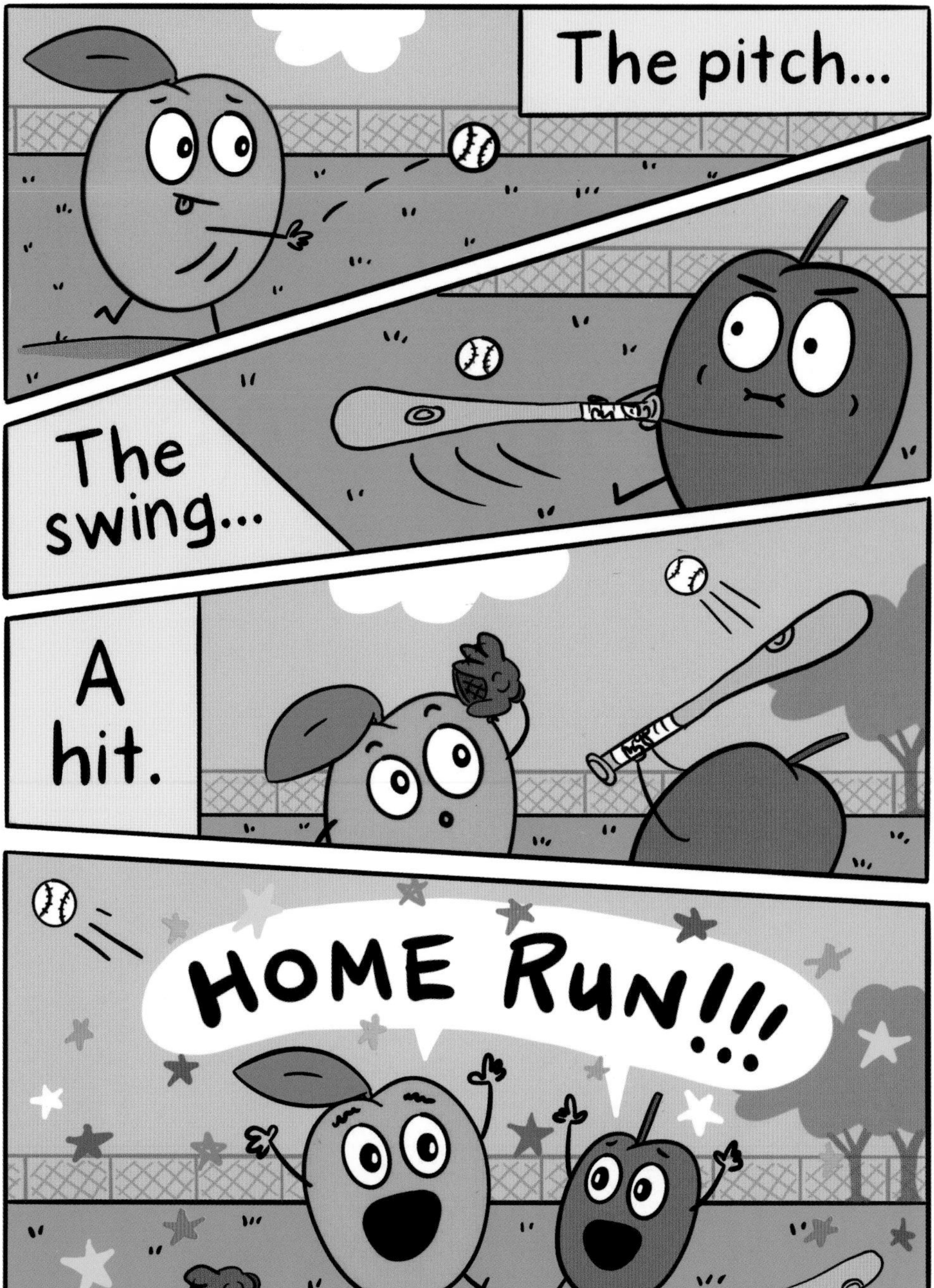
The pitch...
The swing...
A hit.
HOME RUN!!!

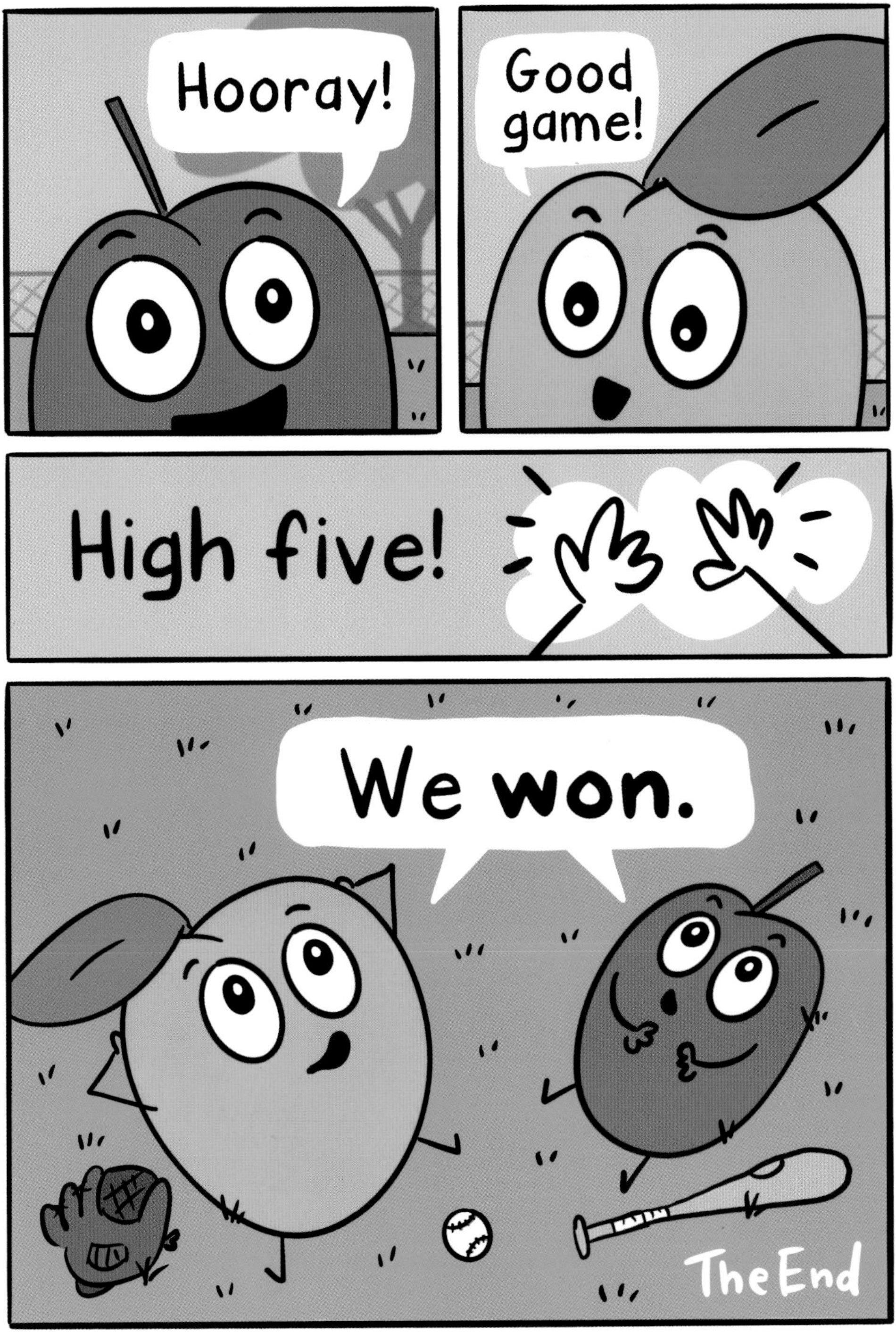
Hooray!
Good game!
High five!
We won.
The End

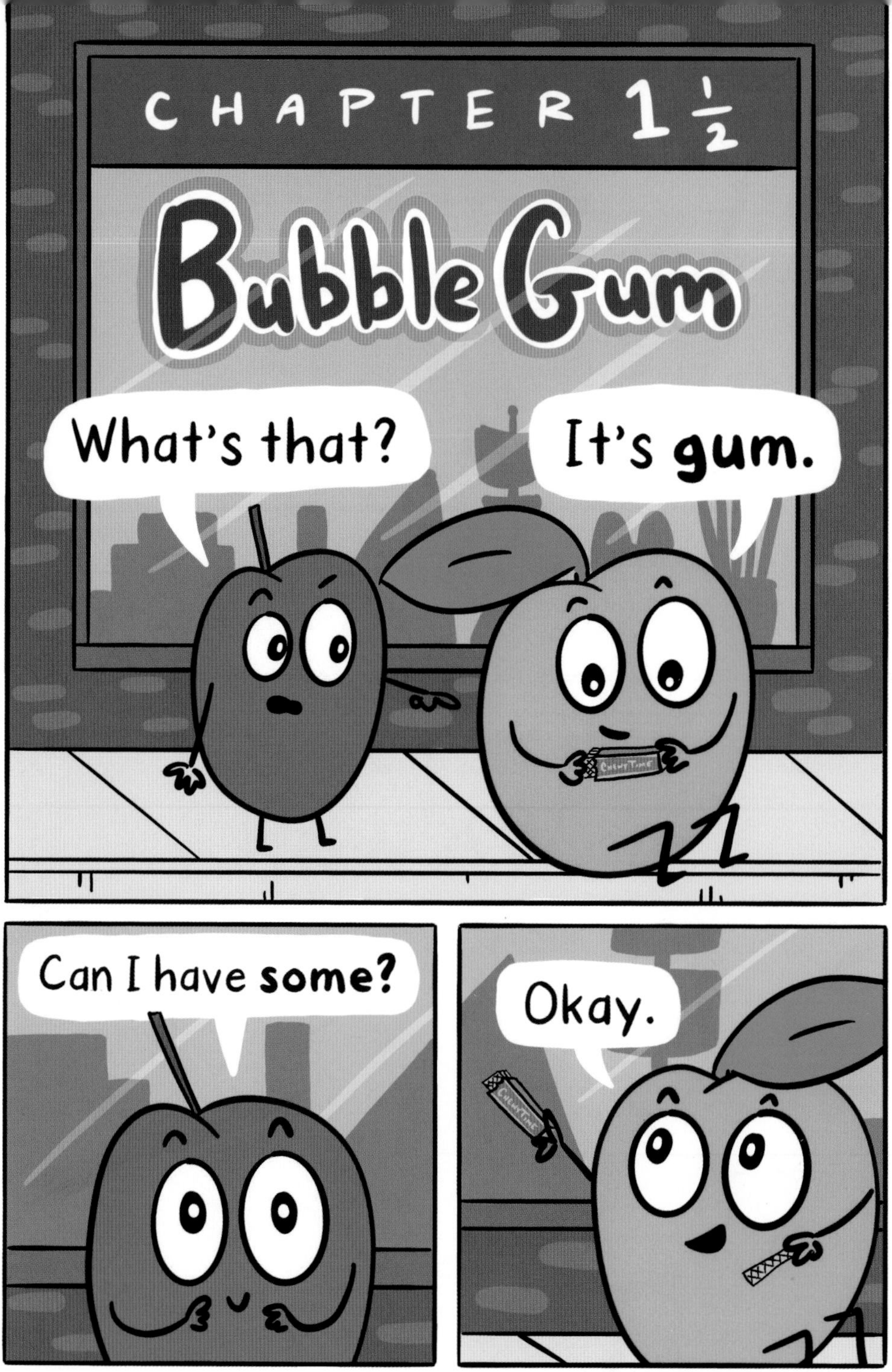
CHAPTER 1 1/2
Bubble Gum
What's that?
It's gum.
Can I have some?
Okay.

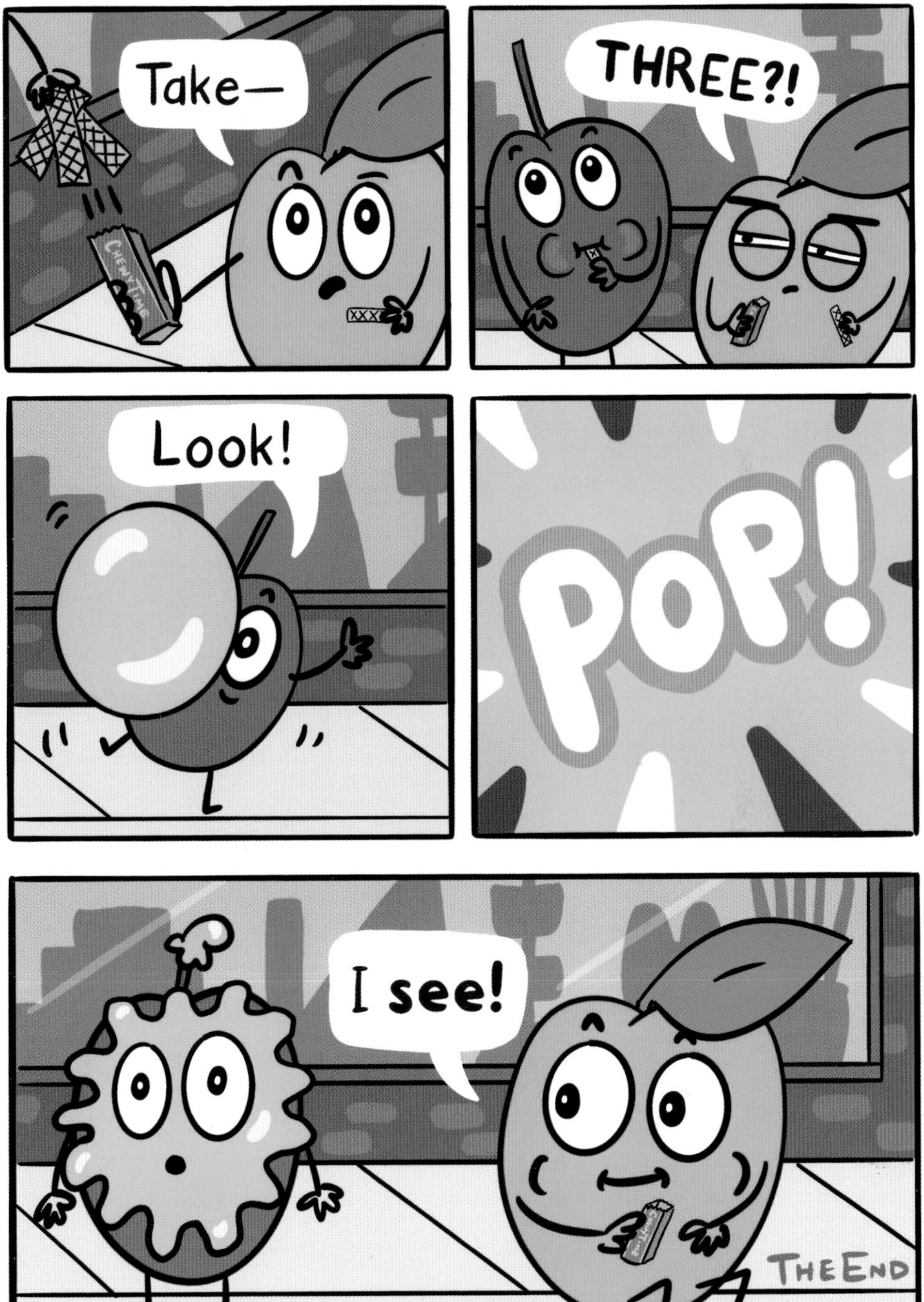
Take—
ChewyTime
THREE?!
Look!
POP!
I see!
ChewyTime
THE END

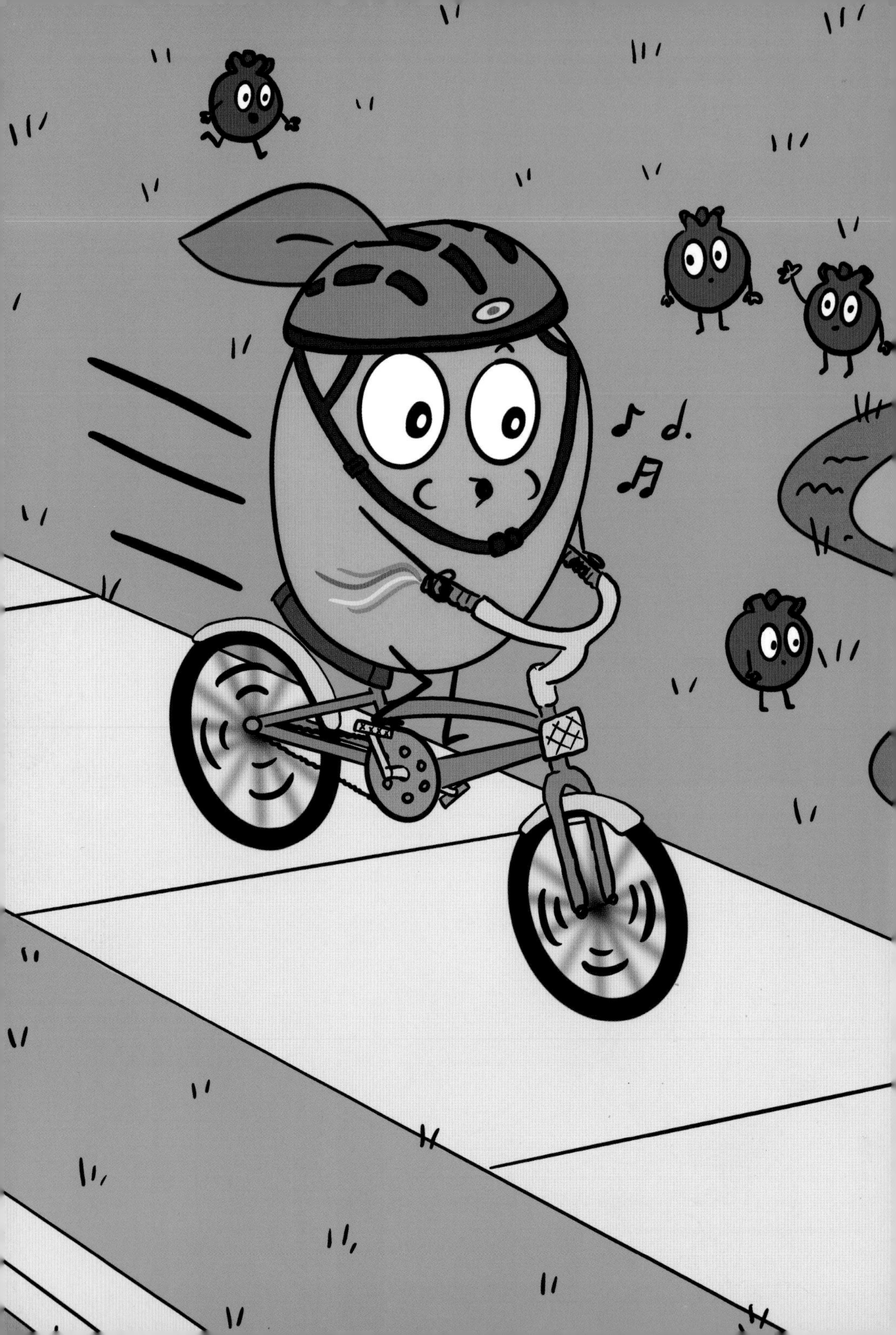

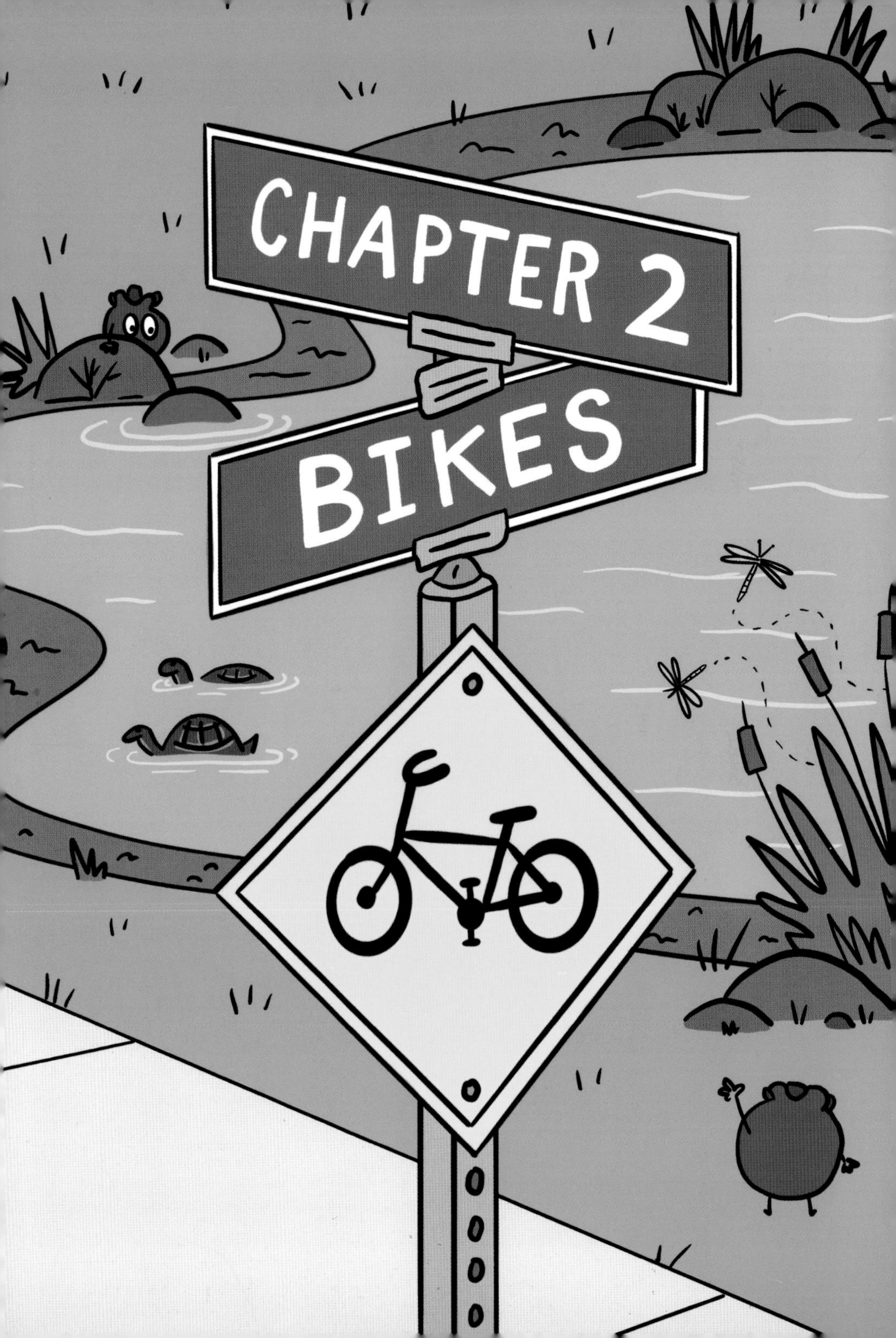
CHAPTER 2
BIKES

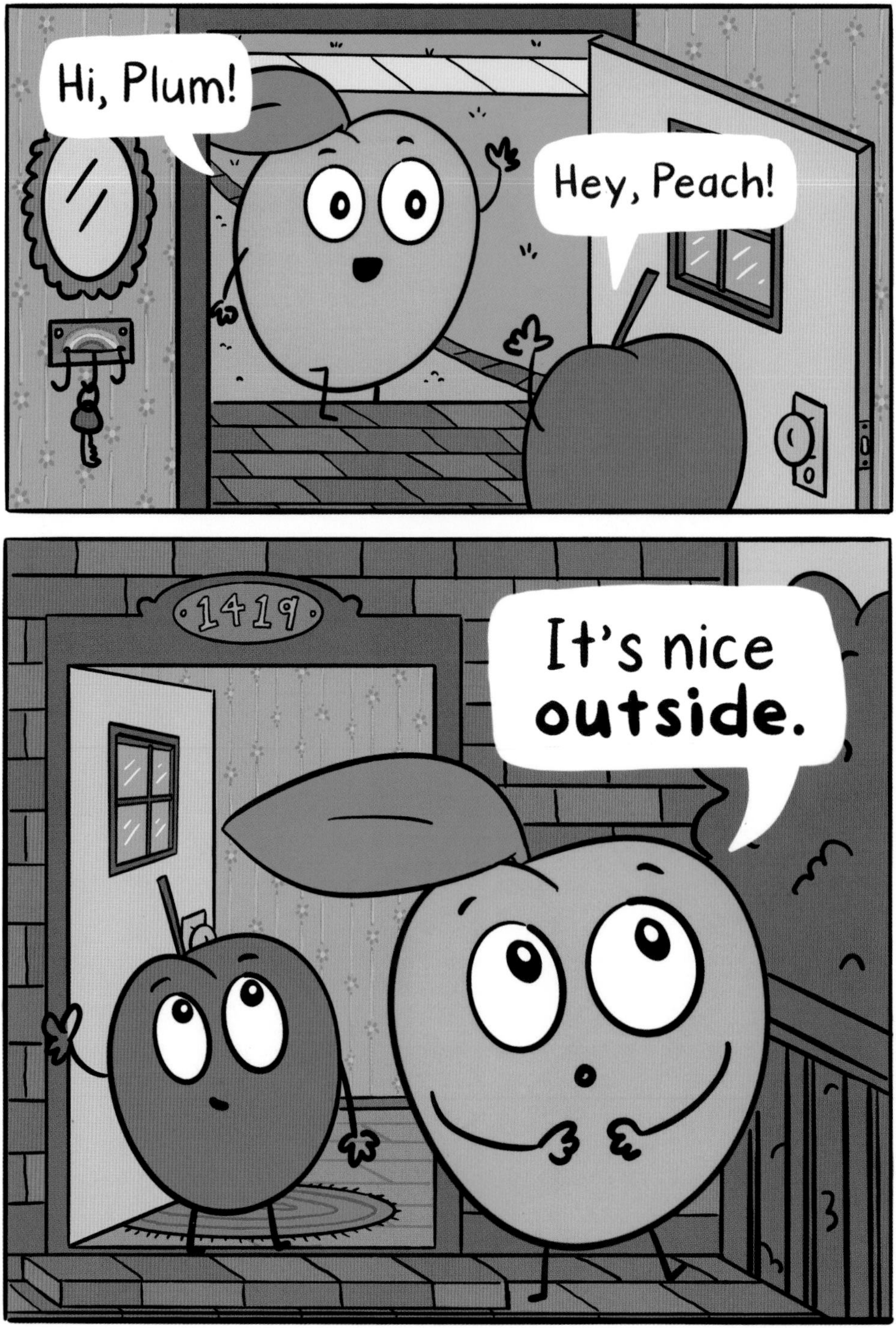
Hi, Plum!
Hey, Peach!
1419
It's nice **outside.**

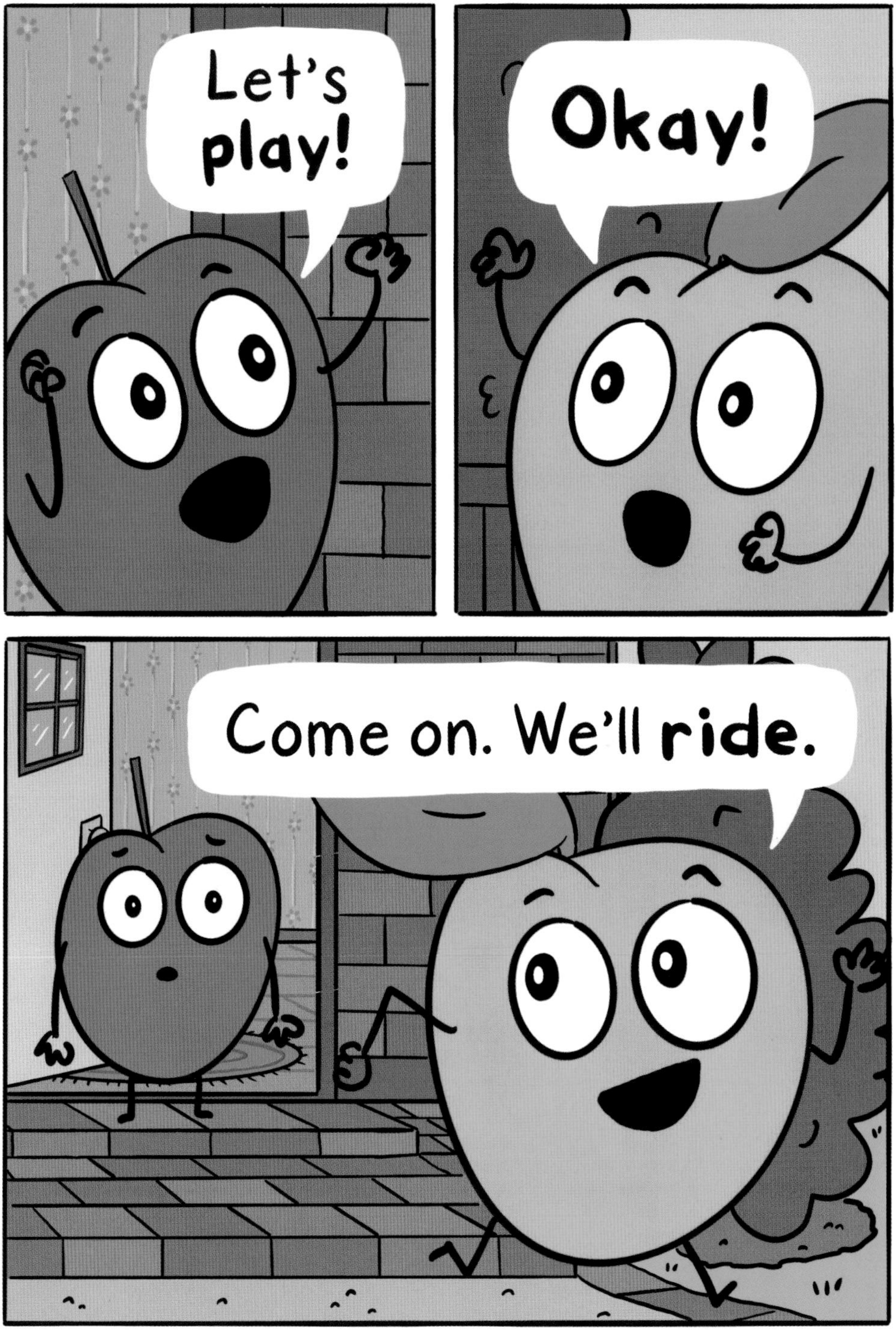
Let's play!
Okay!
Come on. We'll **ride.**

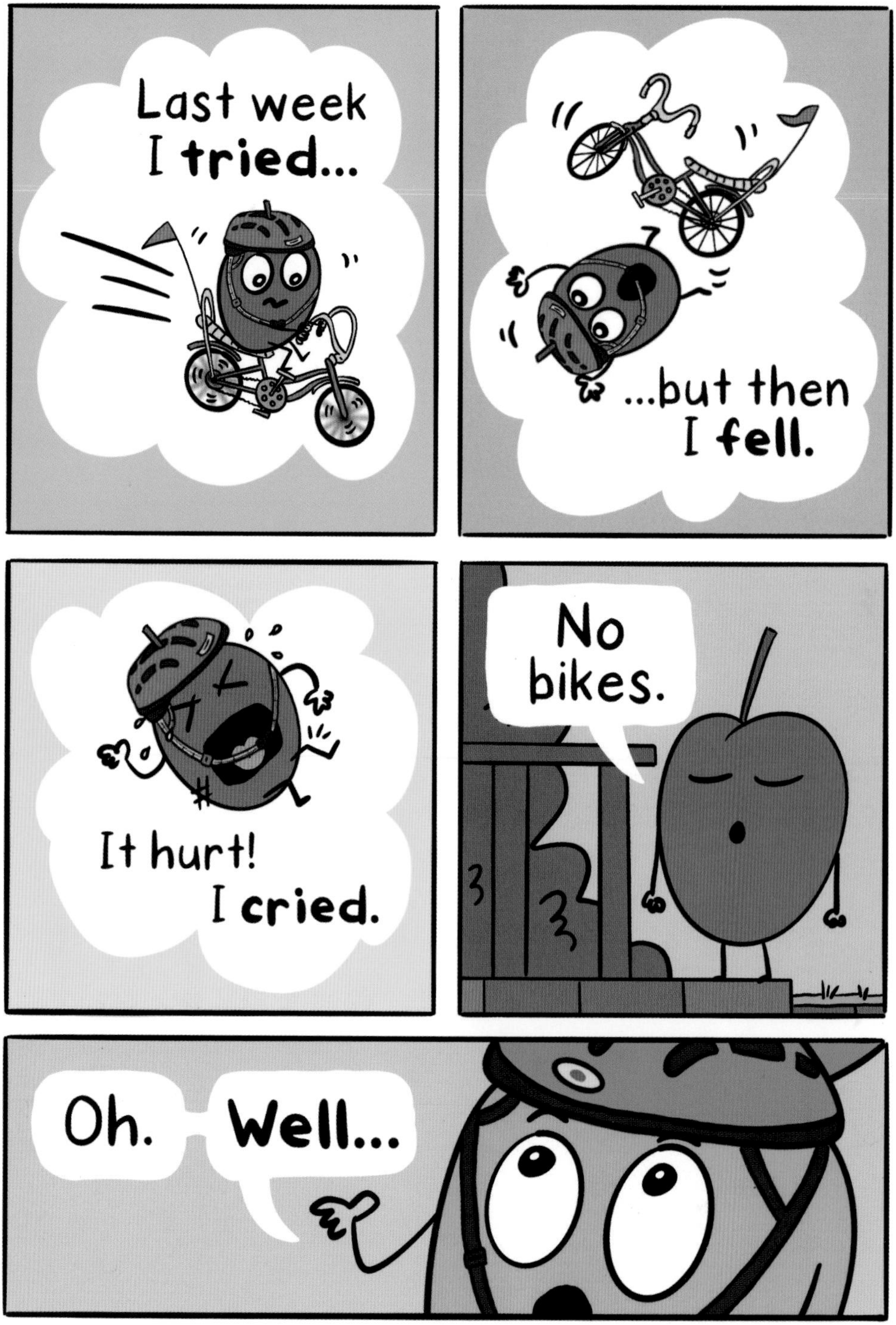
Last week I tried...
...but then I fell.
It hurt! I cried.
No bikes.
Oh.
Well...

33

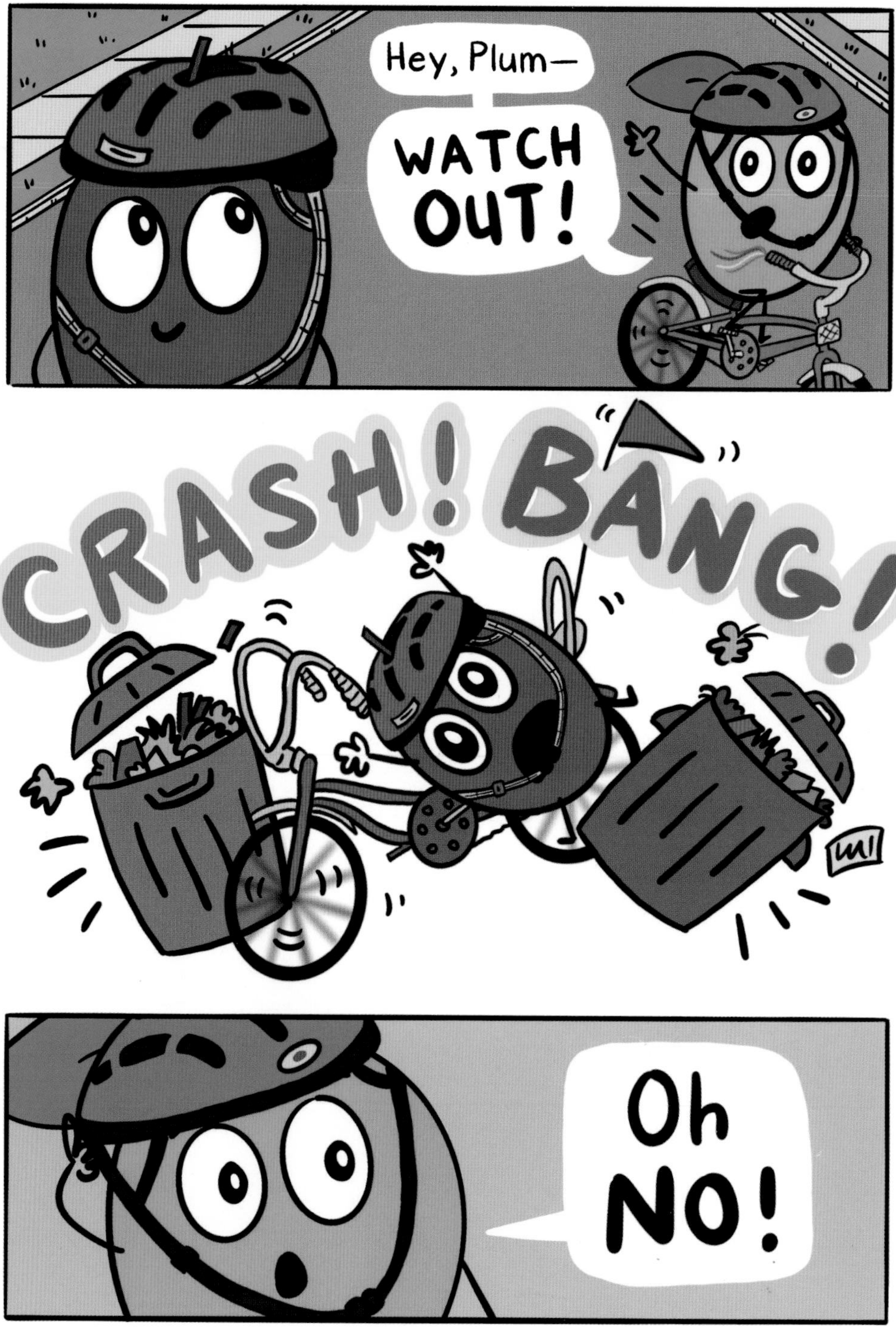
Hey, Plum—
WATCH OUT!
CRASH! BANG!
Oh NO!

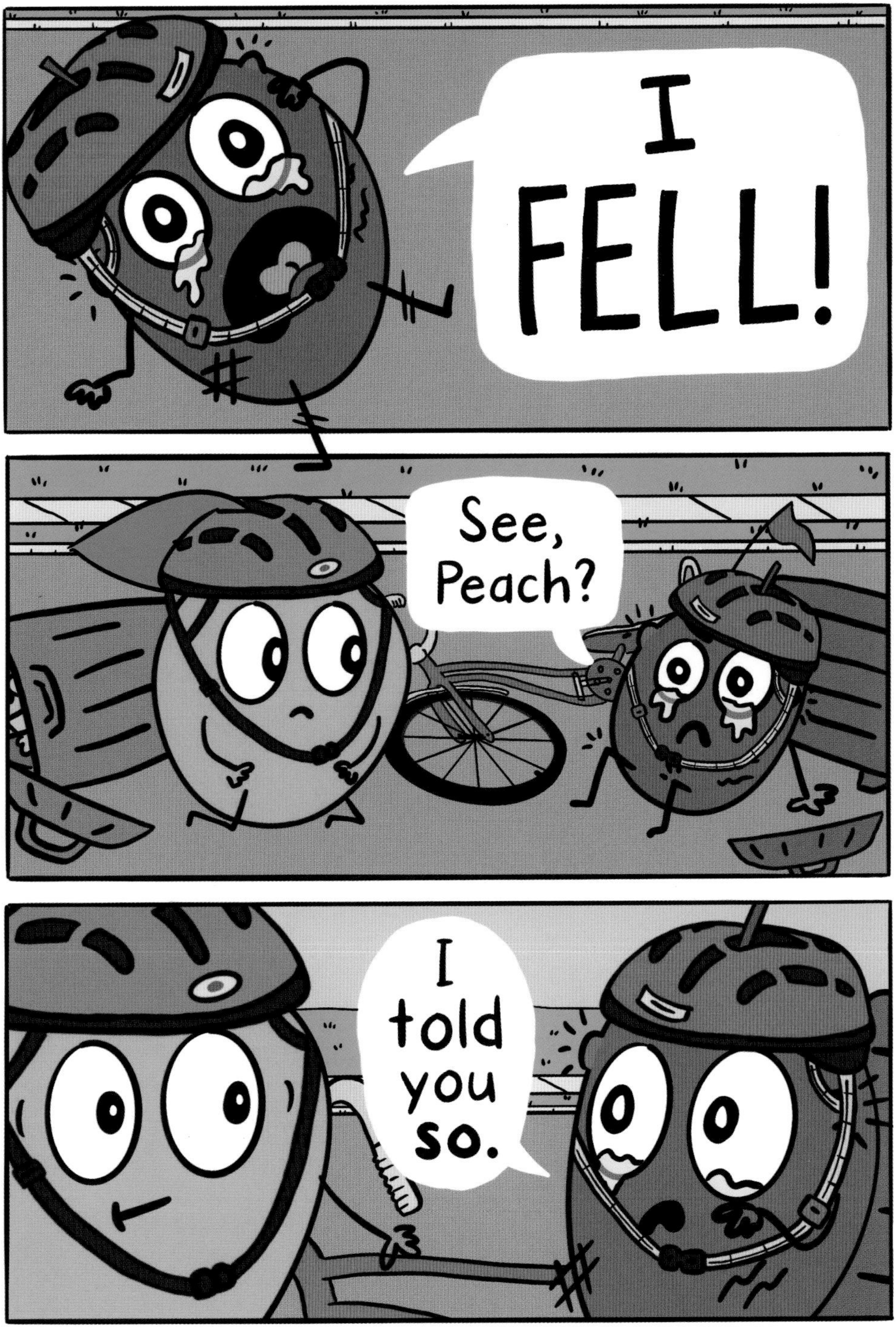
I FELL!
See, Peach?
I told you so.

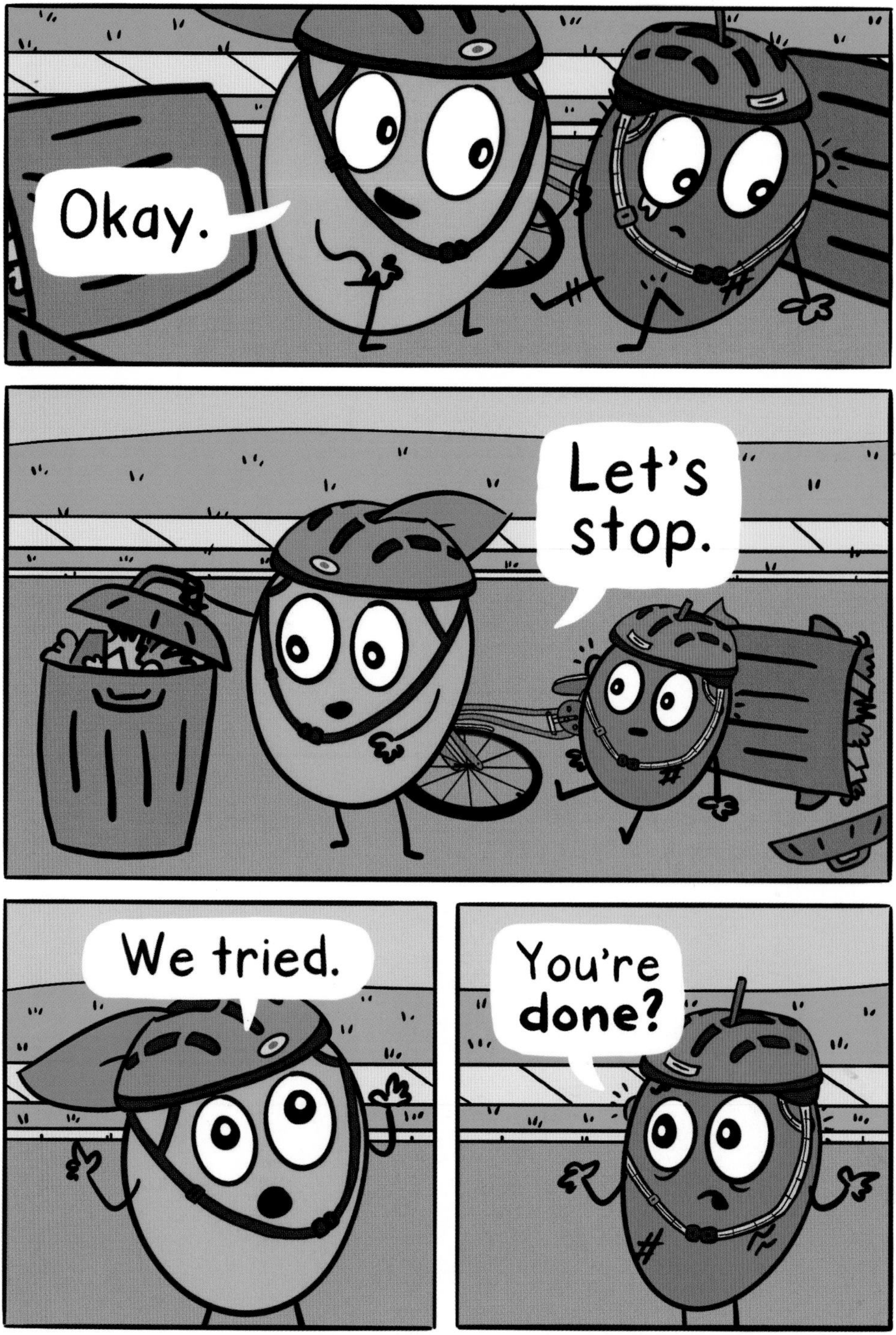
Okay.
Let's stop.
We tried.
You're done?

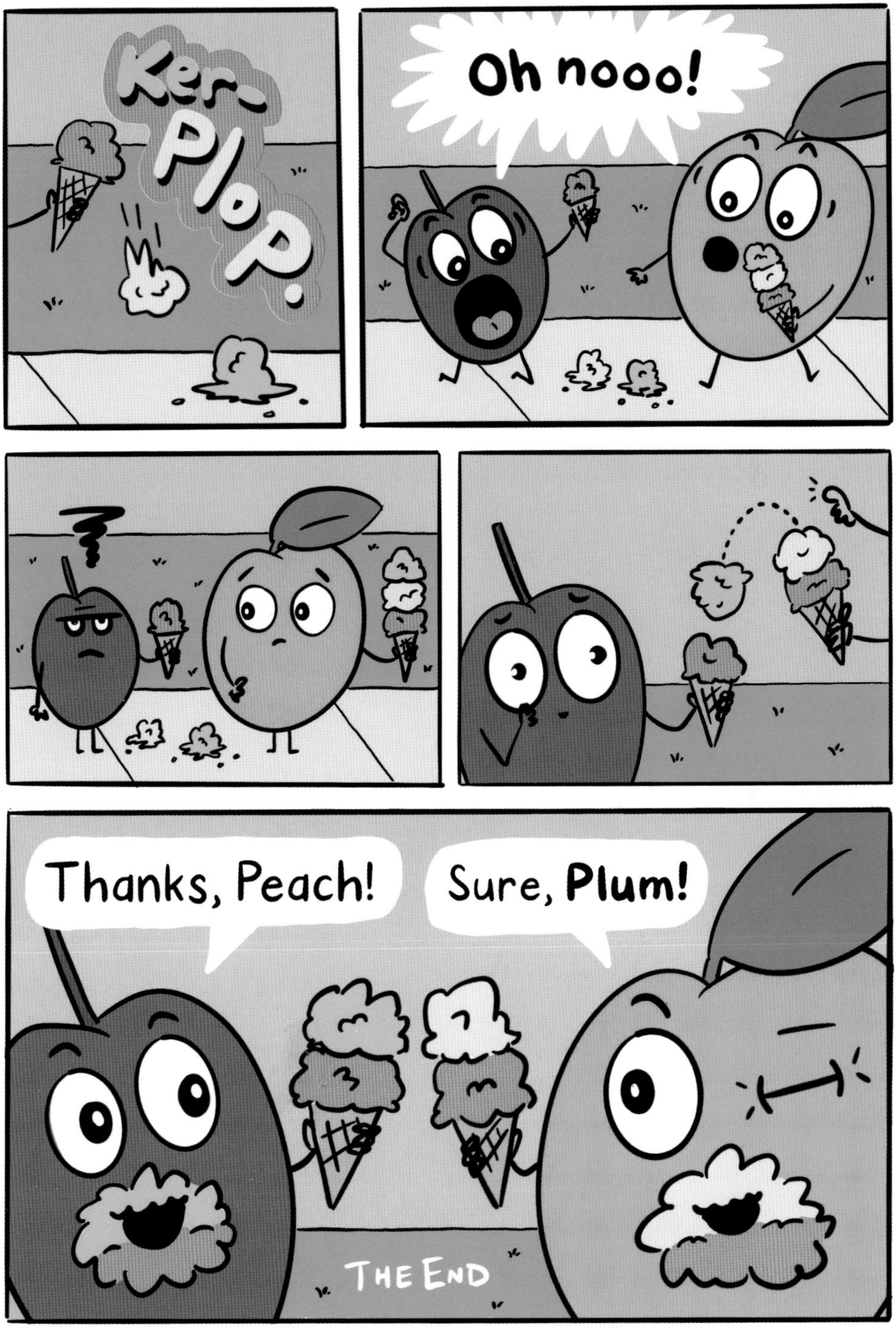
Ker-
Plop.
Oh nooo!
Thanks, Peach!
Sure, Plum!
THE END

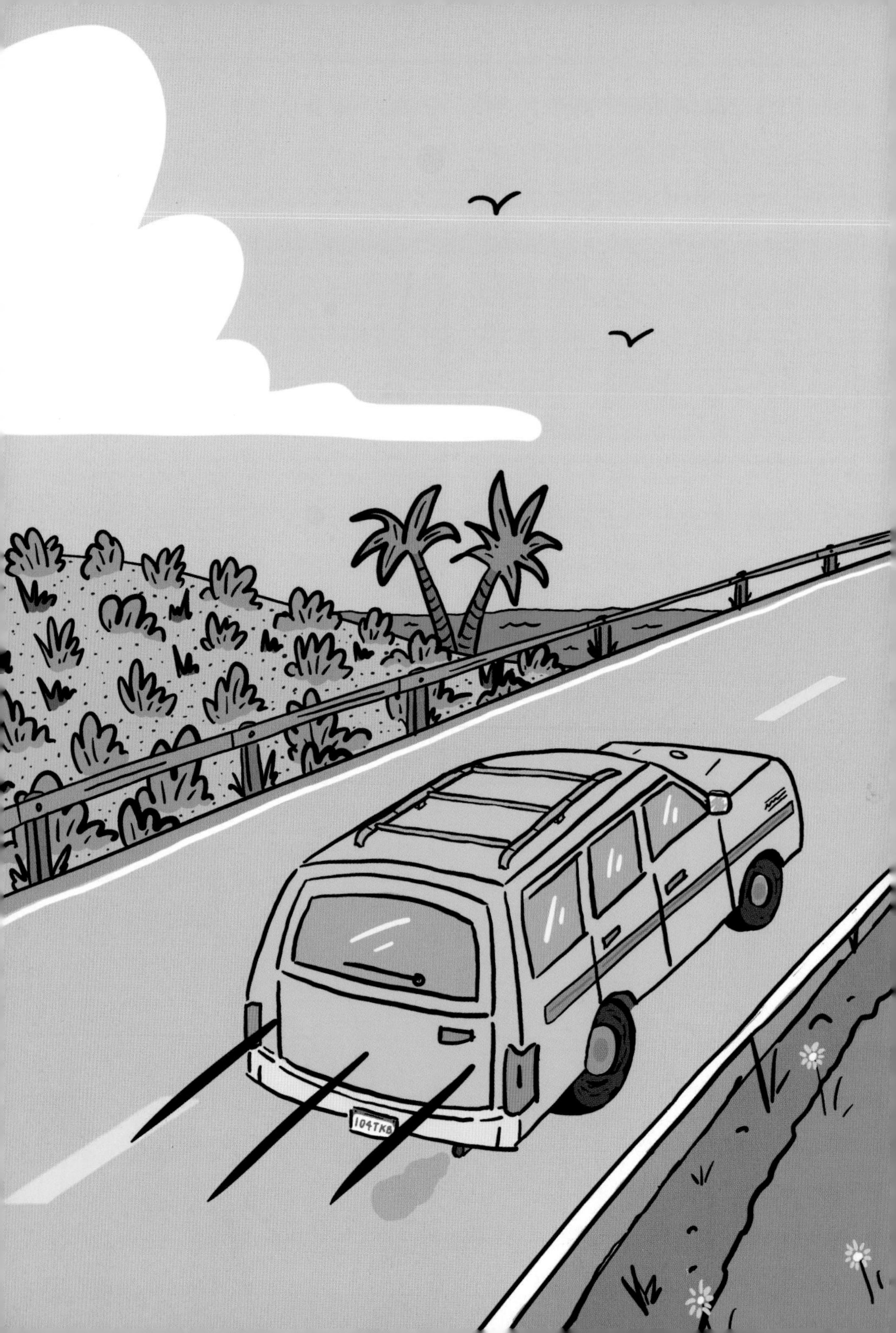
104TKB

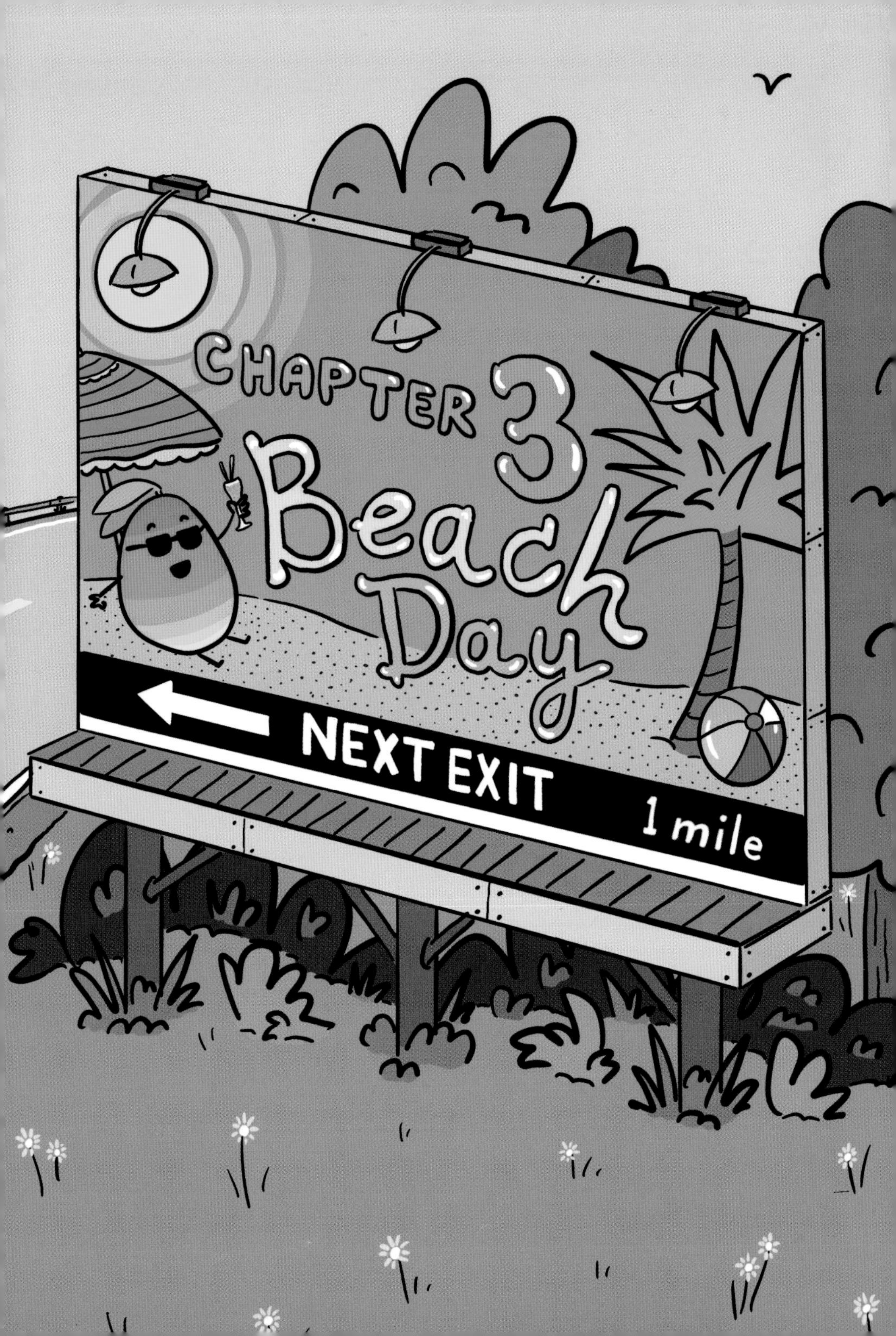
CHAPTER 3
Beach Day
NEXT EXIT
1 mile

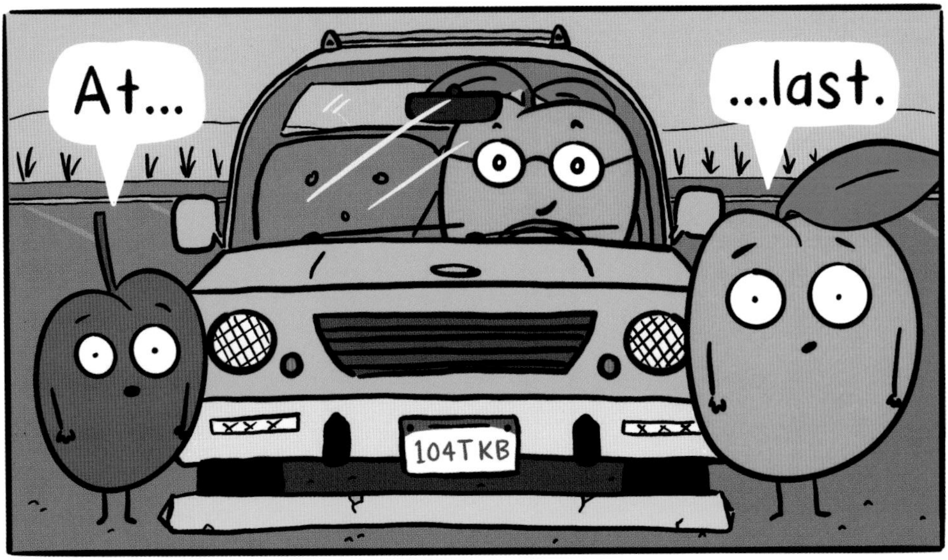
At...
...last.
104TKB

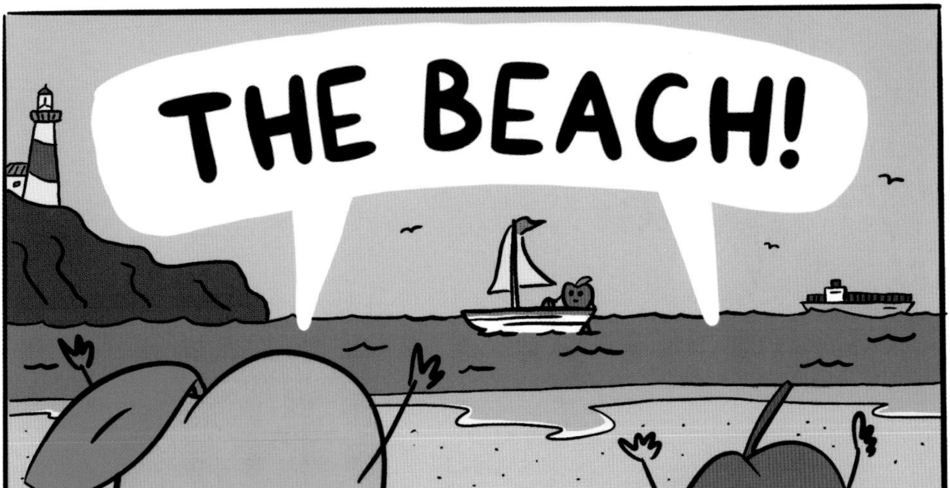
THE BEACH!

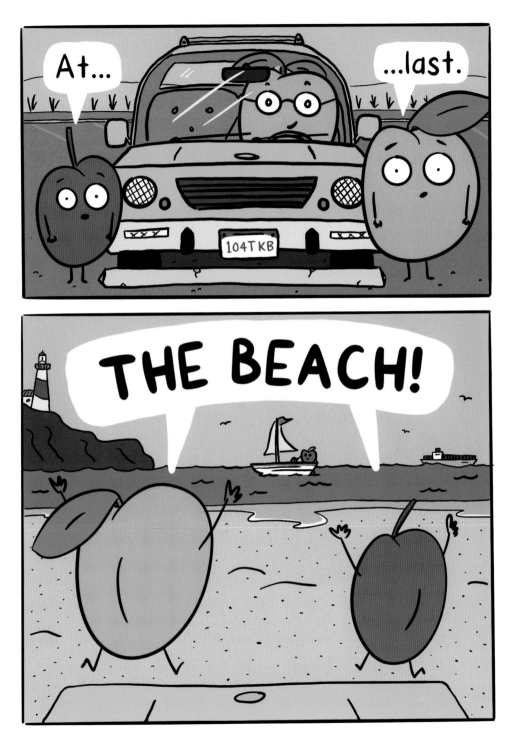

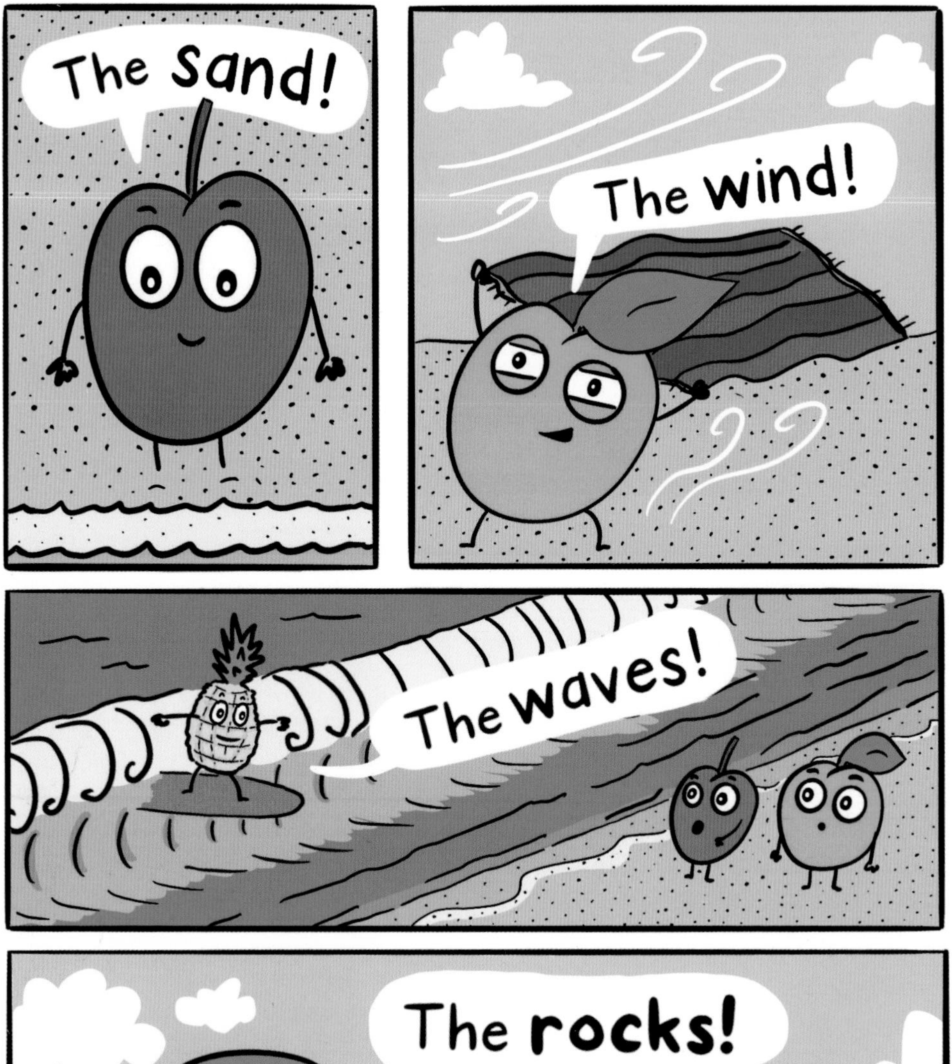
The Sand!
The wind!
The waves!
The rocks!

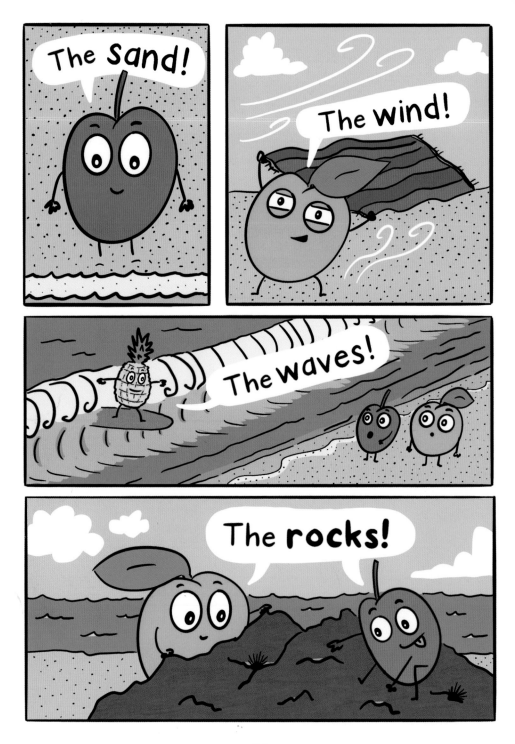

52

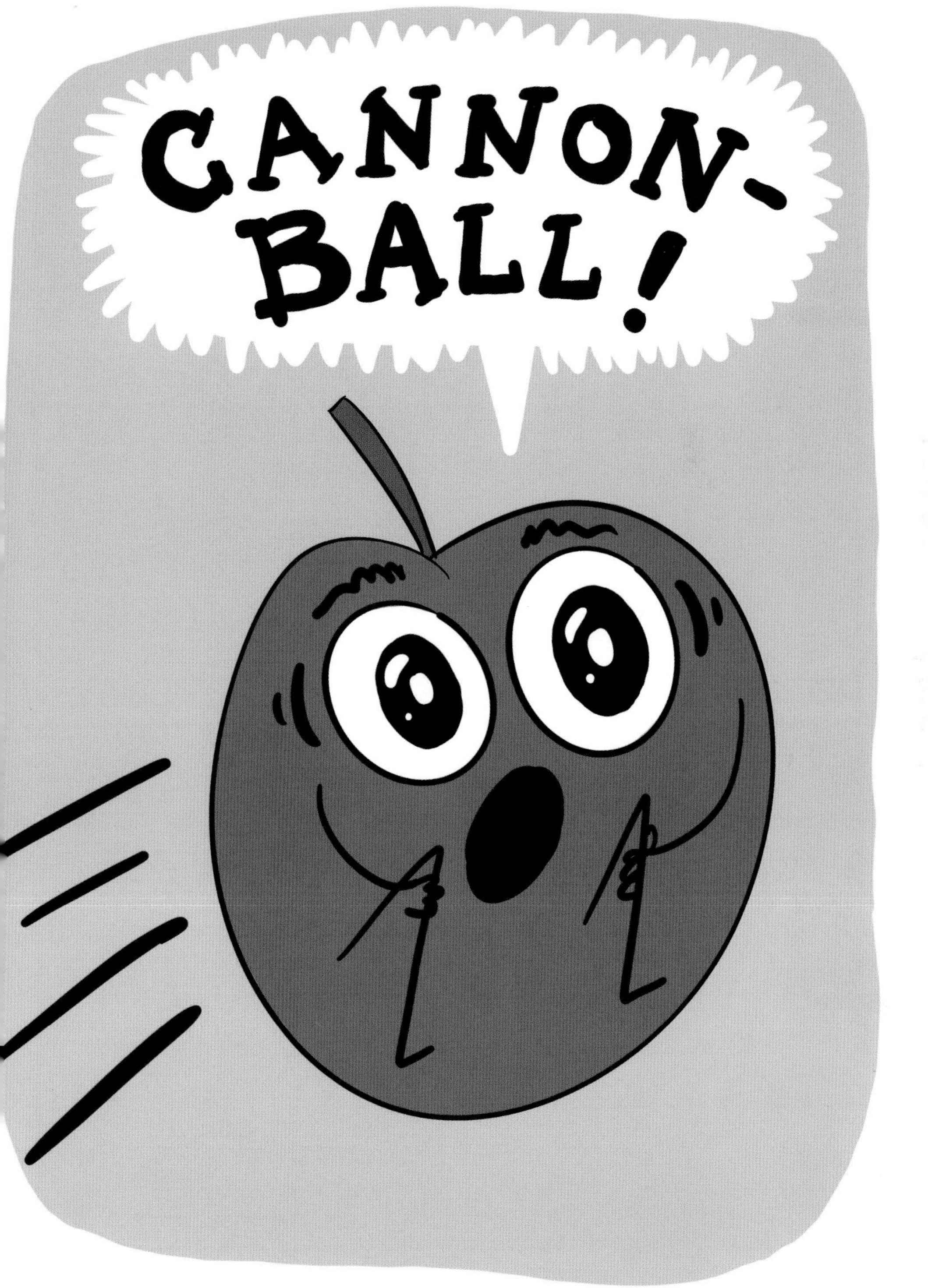
CANNON-
BALL!

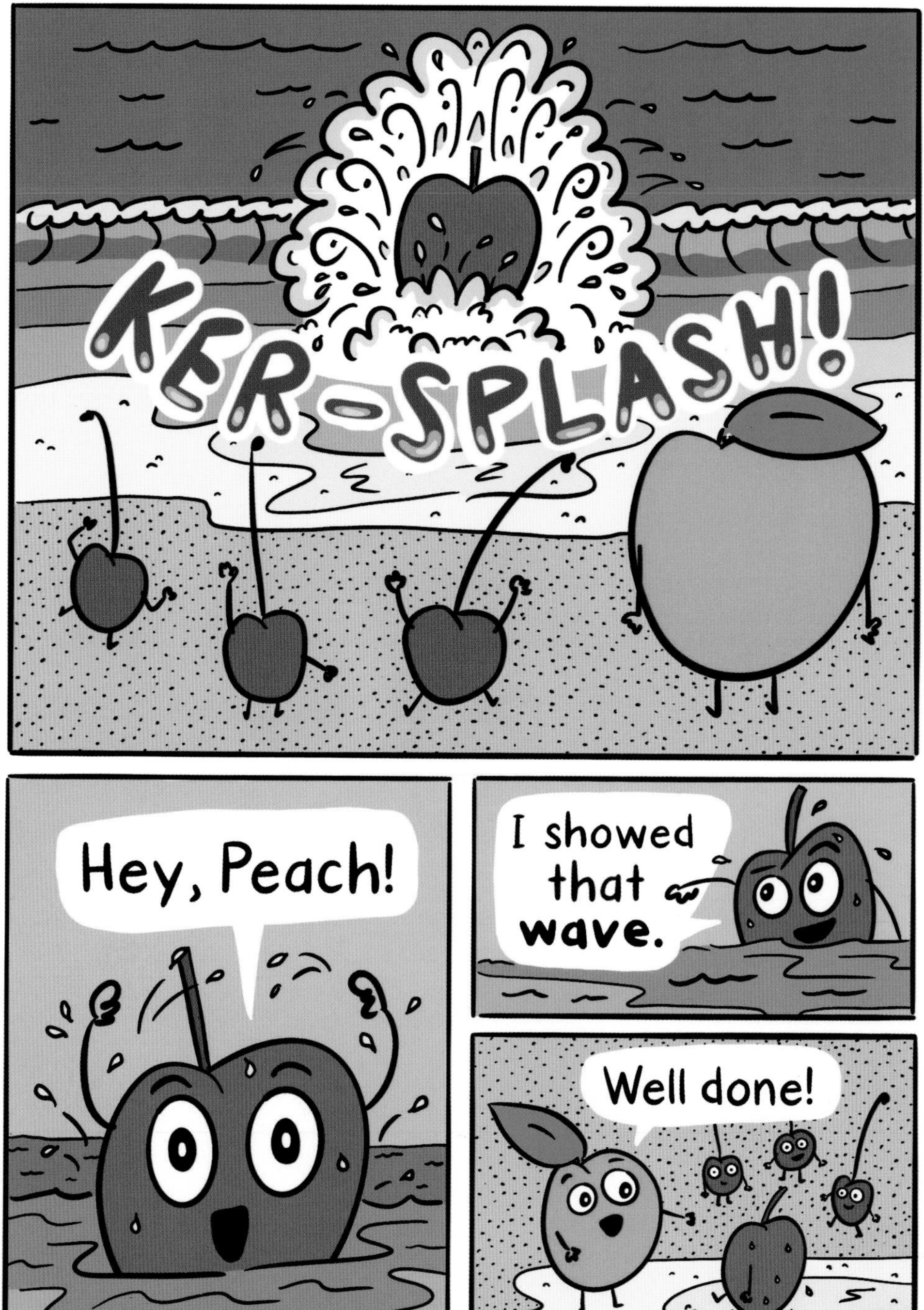
KER-SPLASH!
Hey, Peach!
I showed that wave.
Well done!

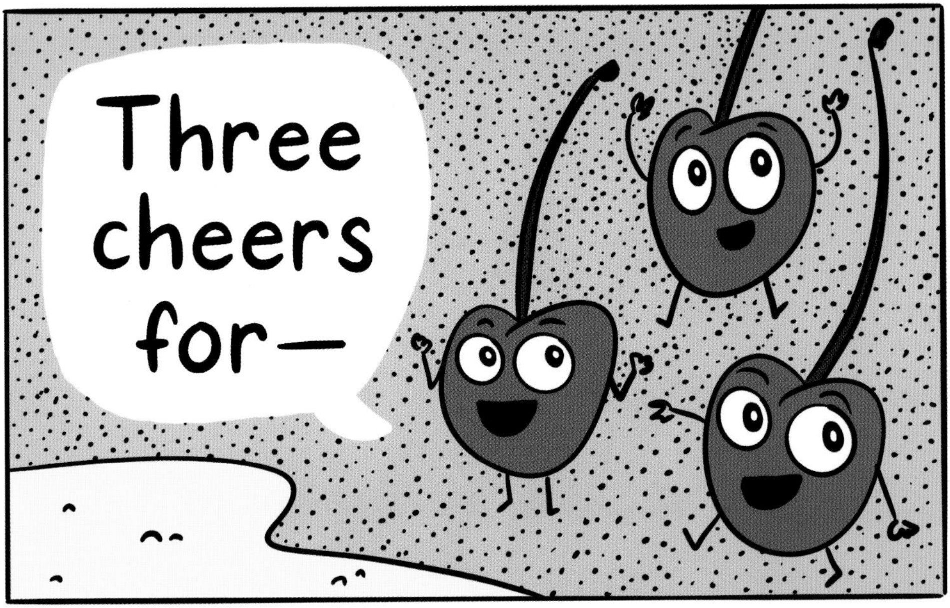
Three cheers for—

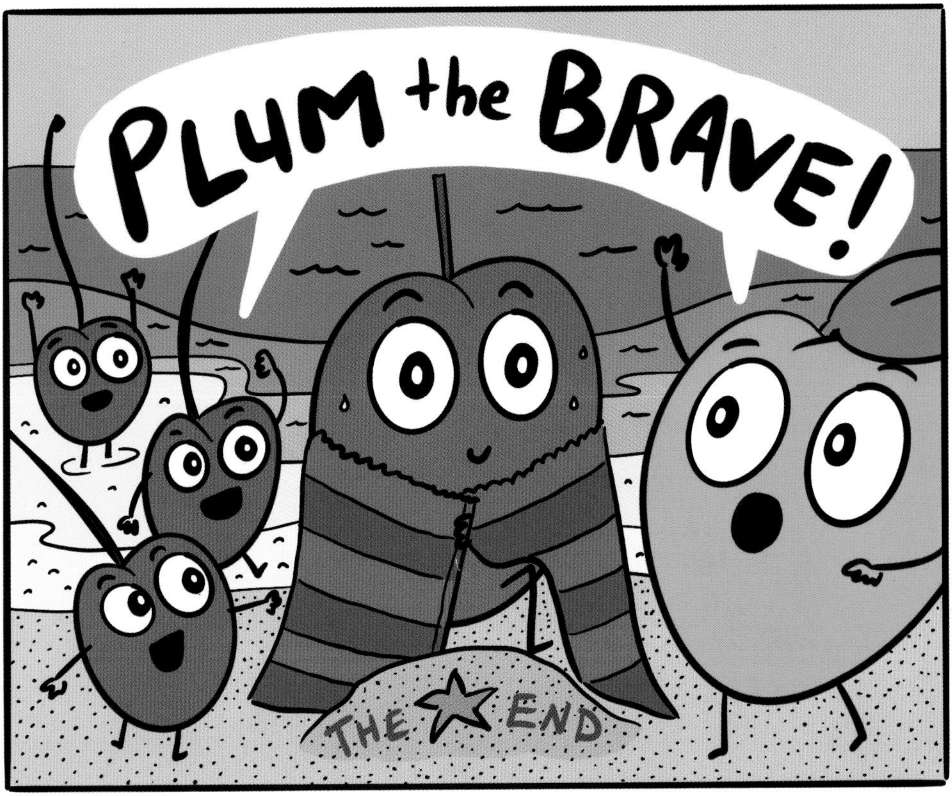
PLUM the BRAVE!
THE END

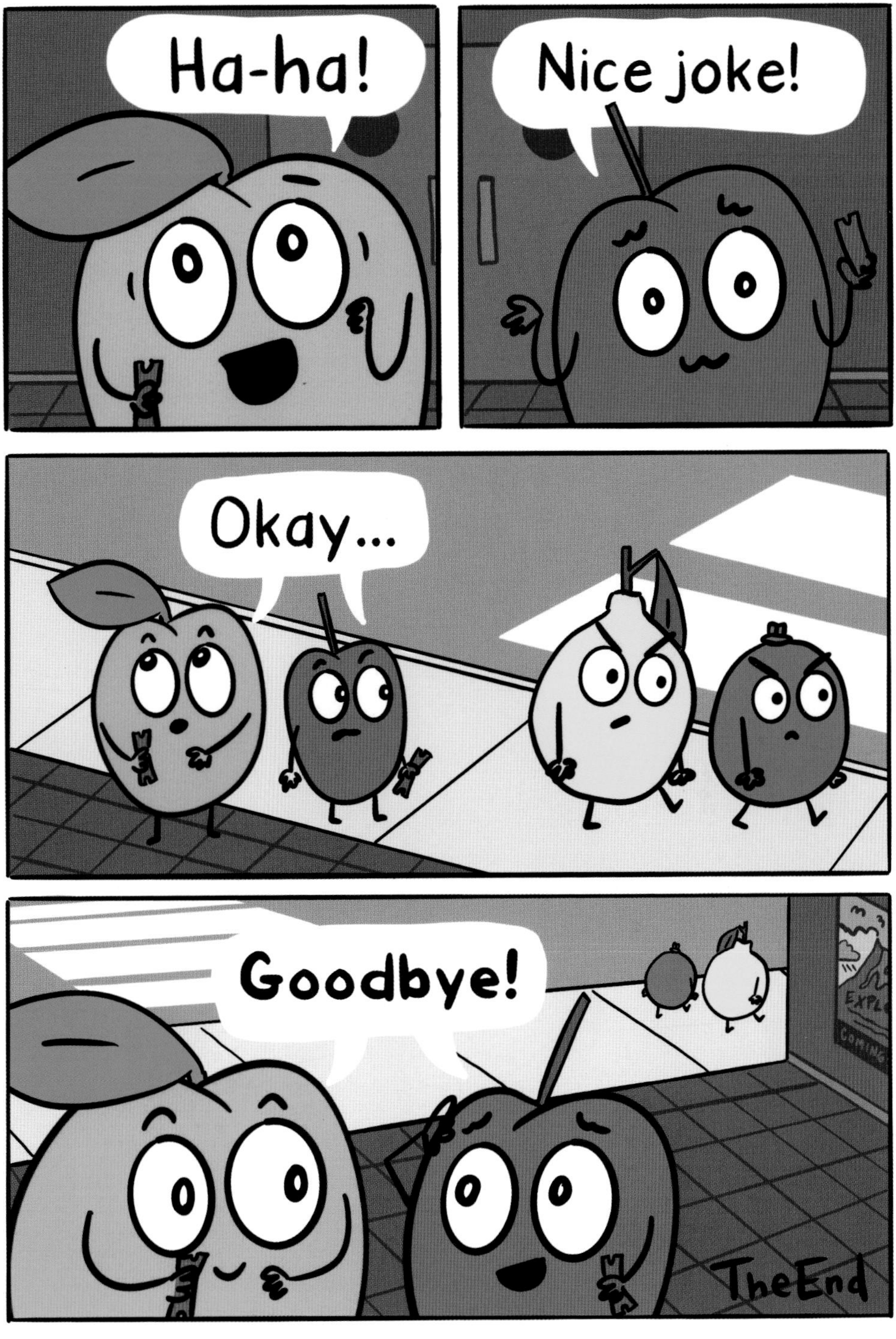
Ha-ha!
Nice joke!
Okay...
Goodbye!
TheEnd

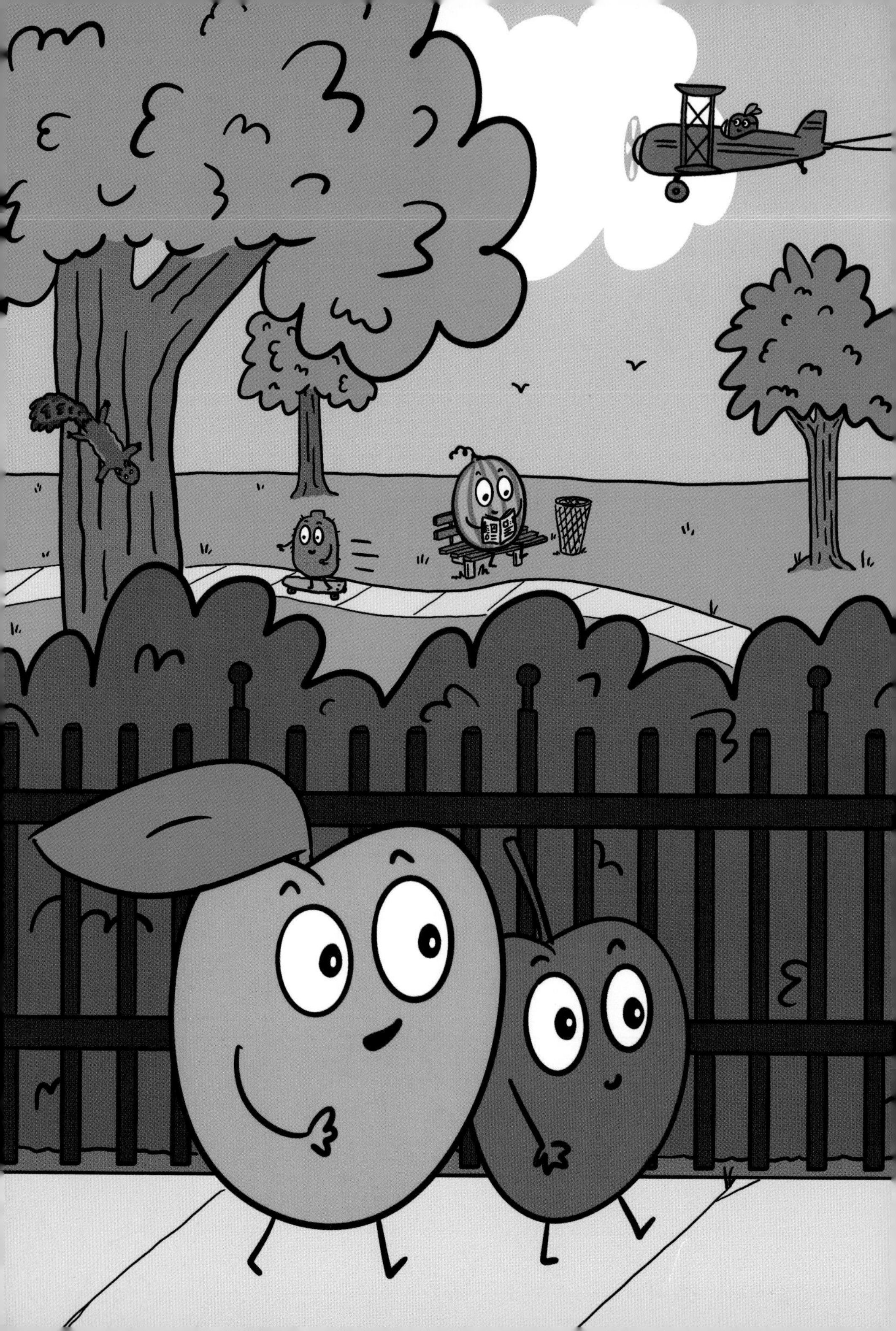

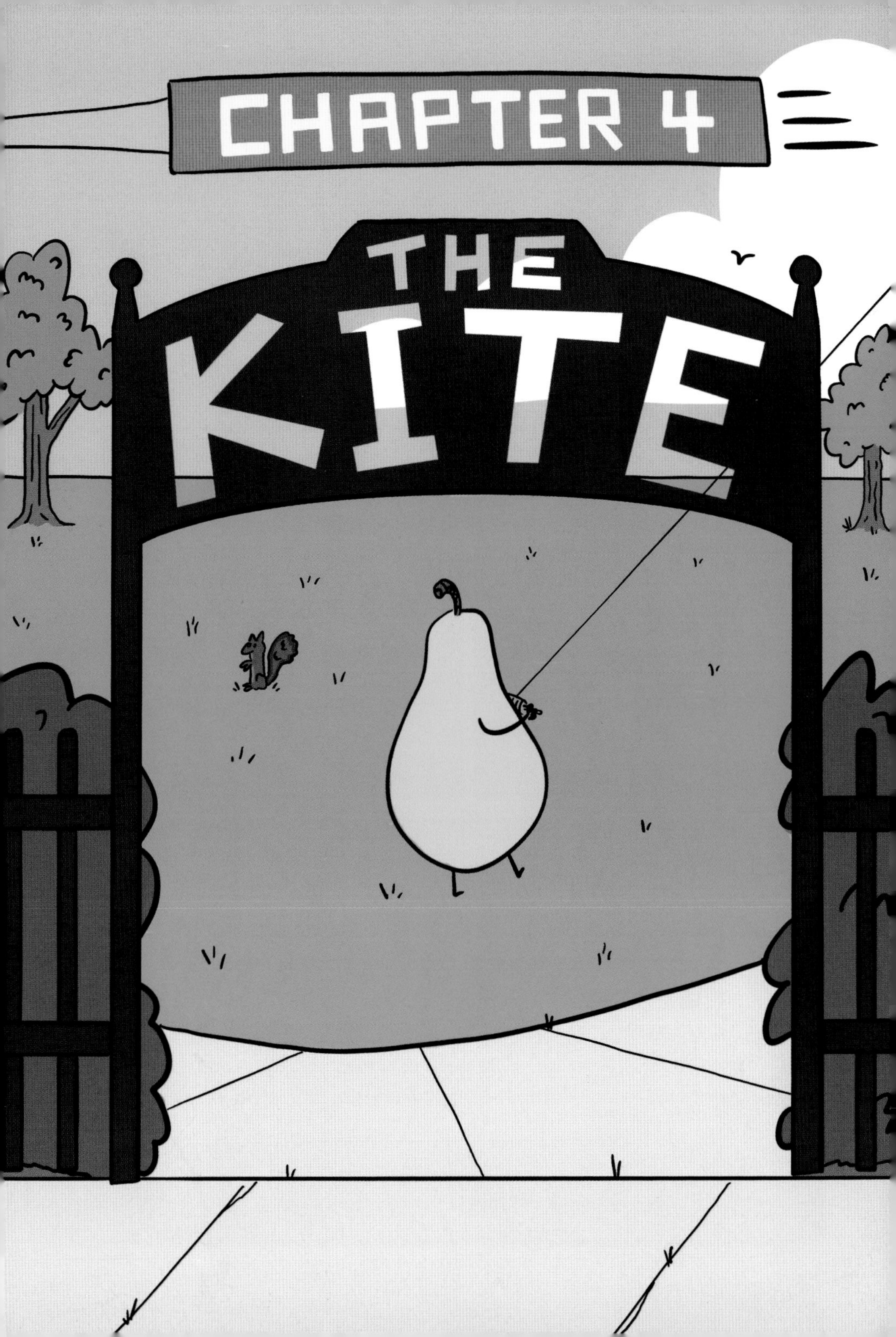
CHAPTER 4
THE KITE

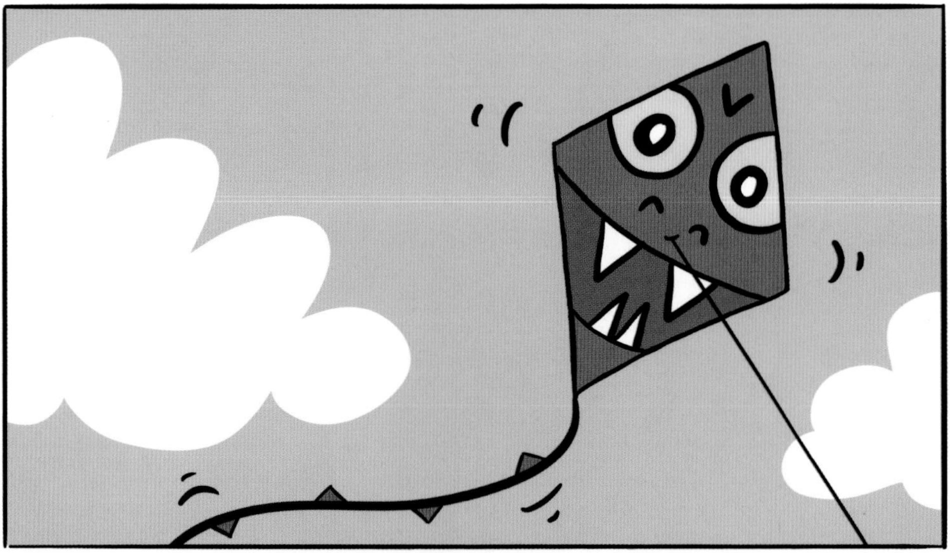

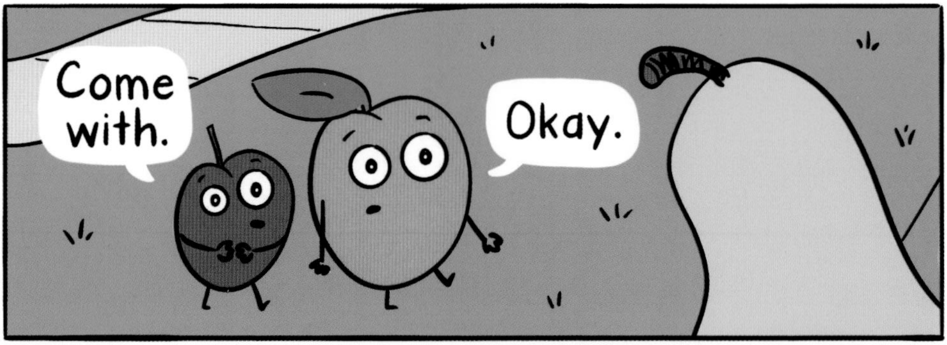

Come with.
Okay.

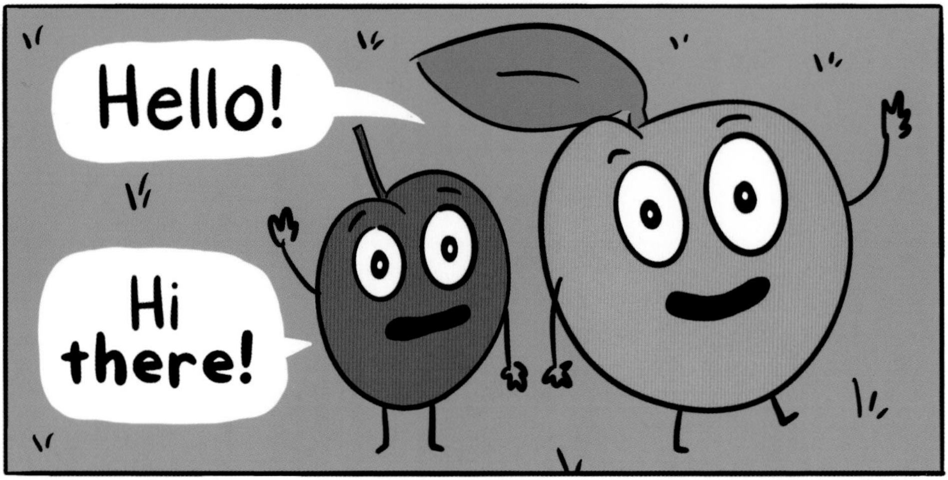

Hello!
Hi there!

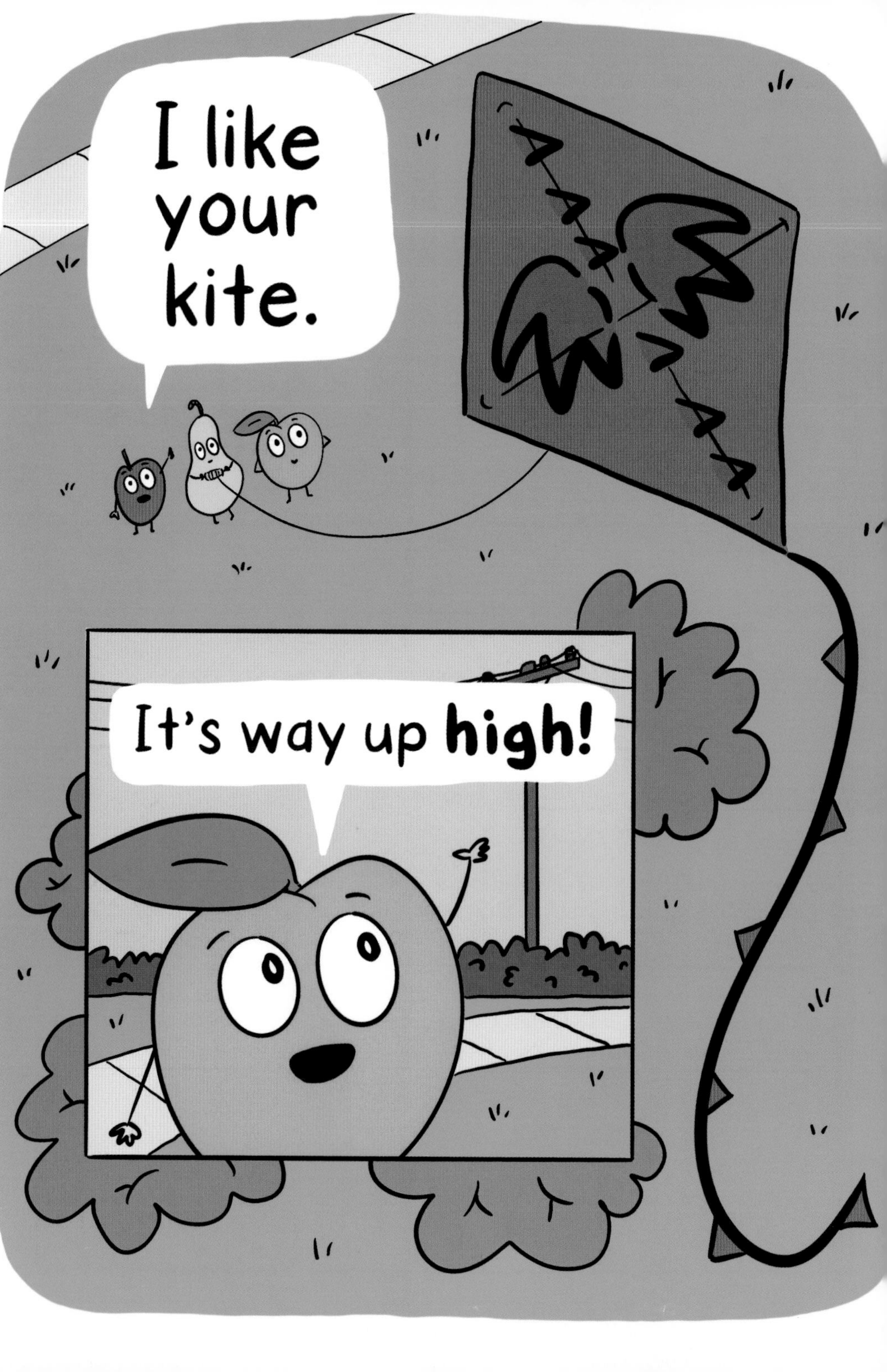
I like your kite.
It's way up **high**!

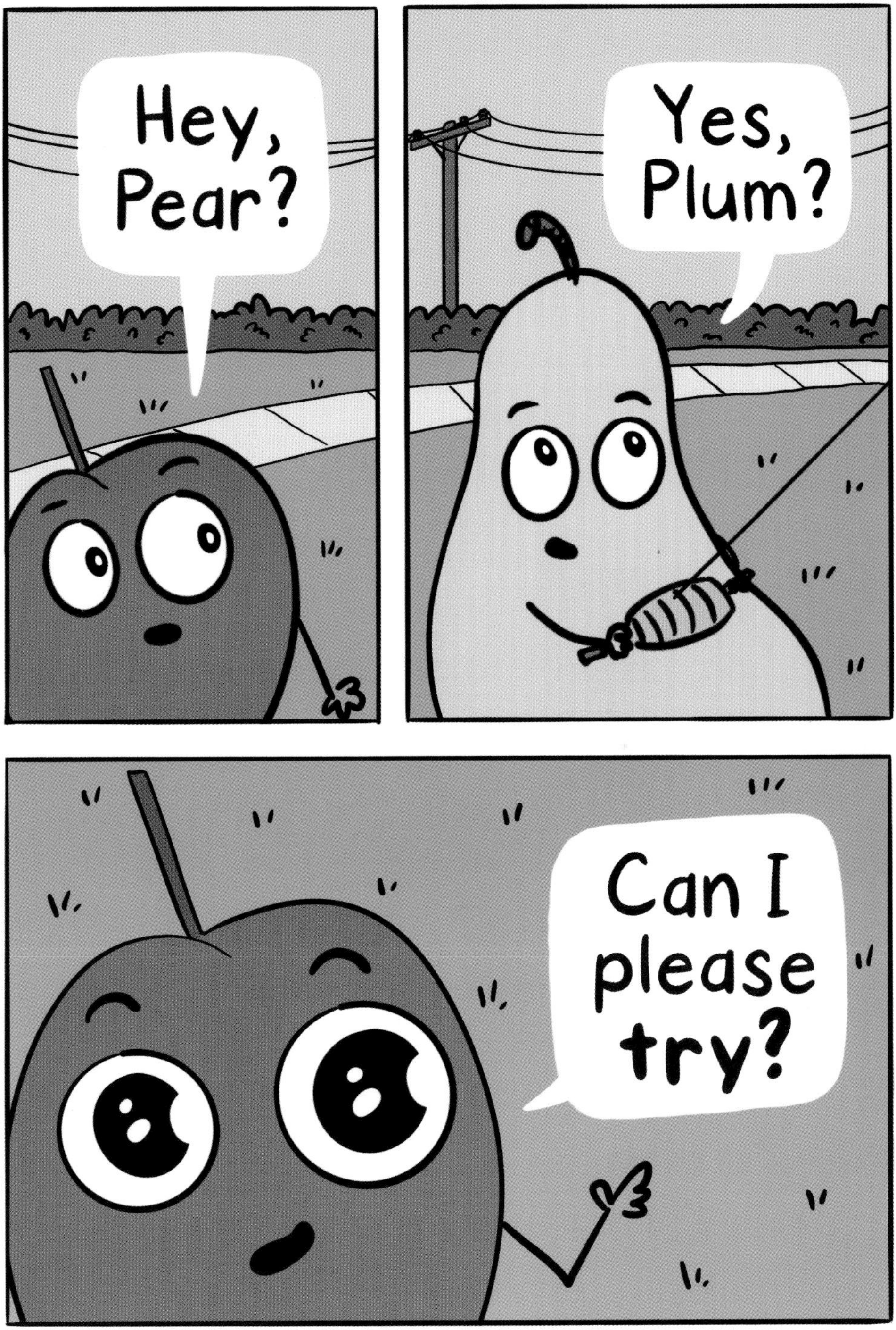
Hey, Pear?
Yes, Plum?
Can I please **try**?

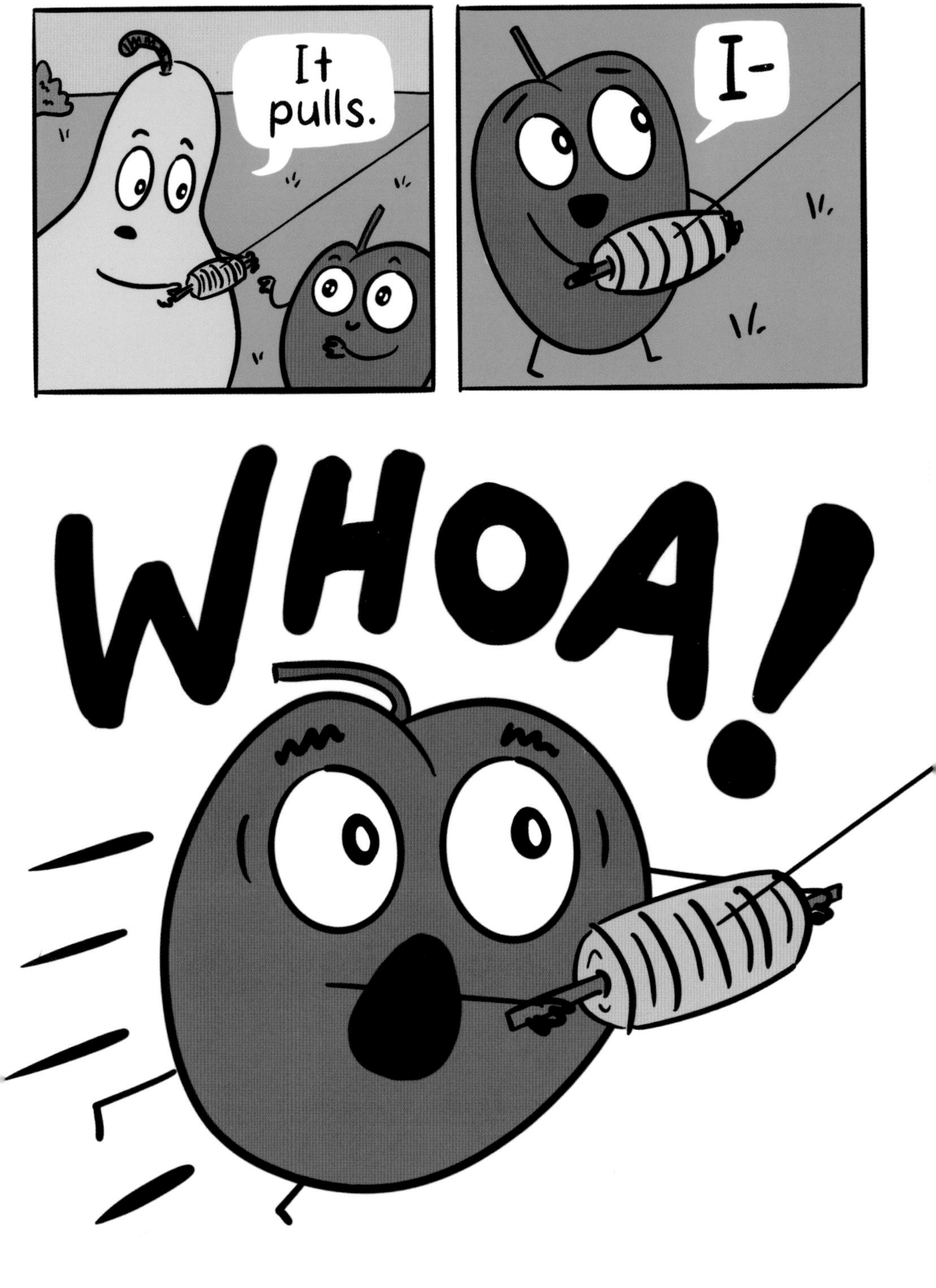
It pulls.
I-
WHOA!

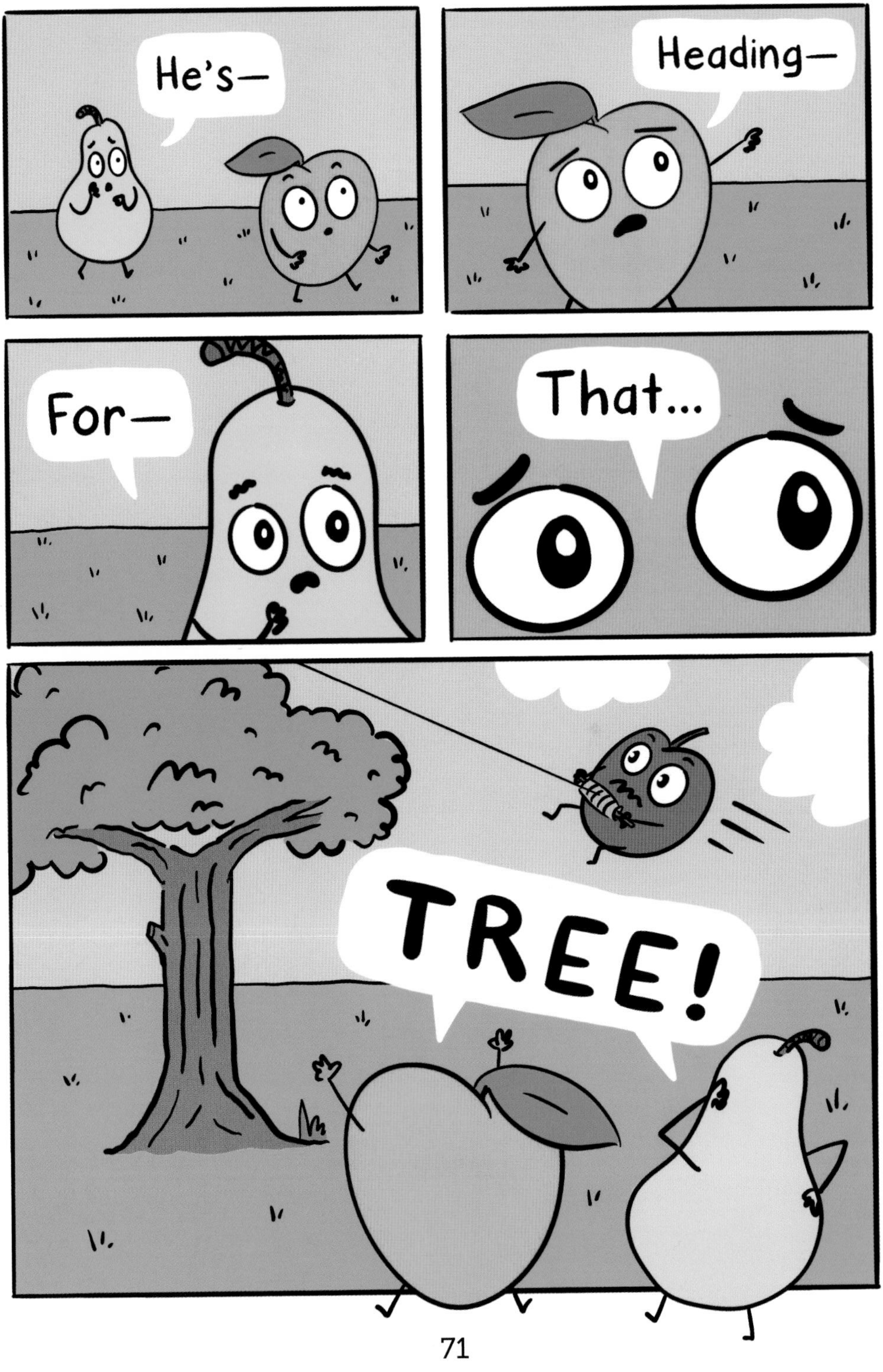
He's—
Heading—
For—
That...
TREE!

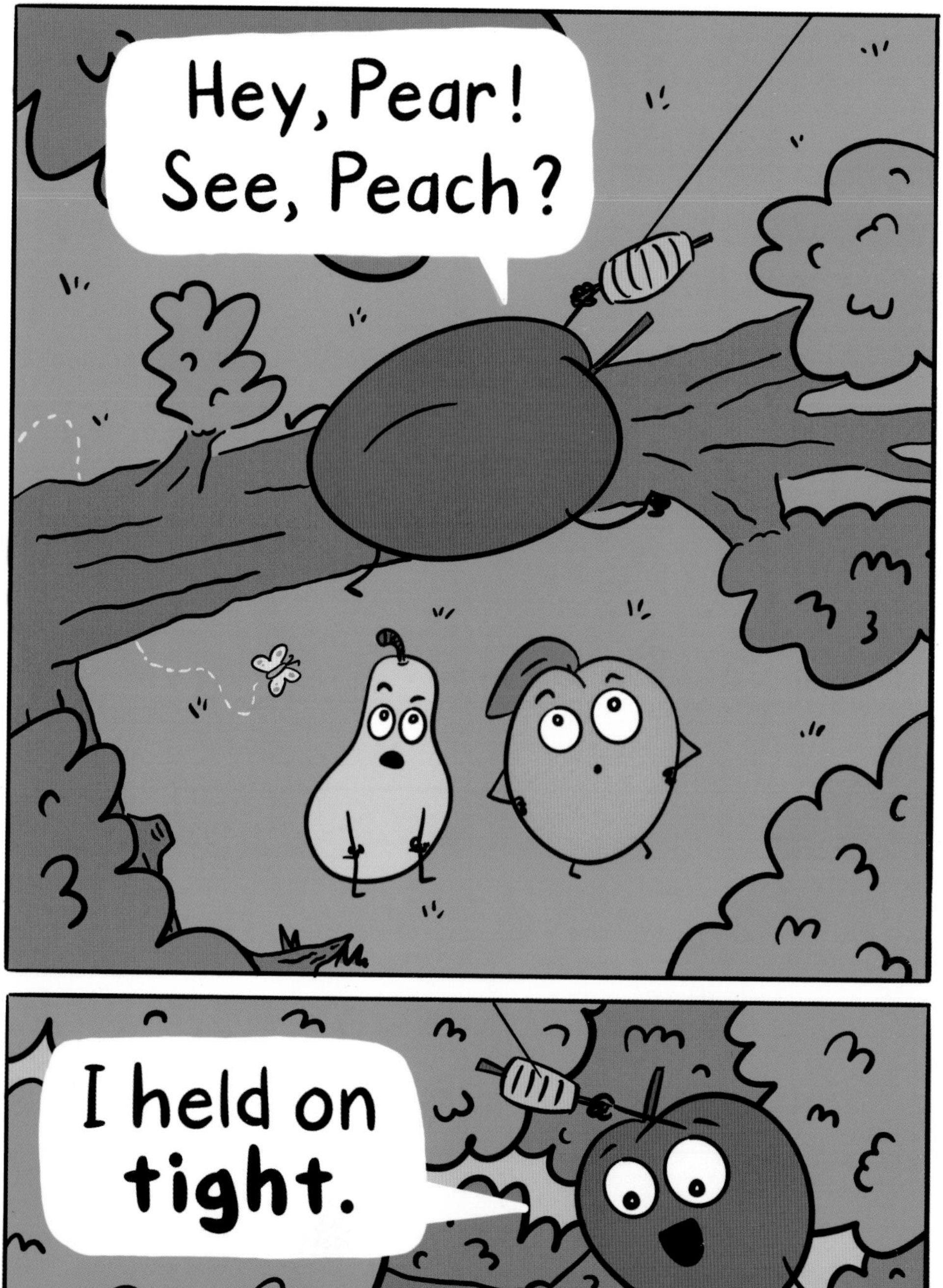
Hey, Pear! See, Peach?
I held on tight.

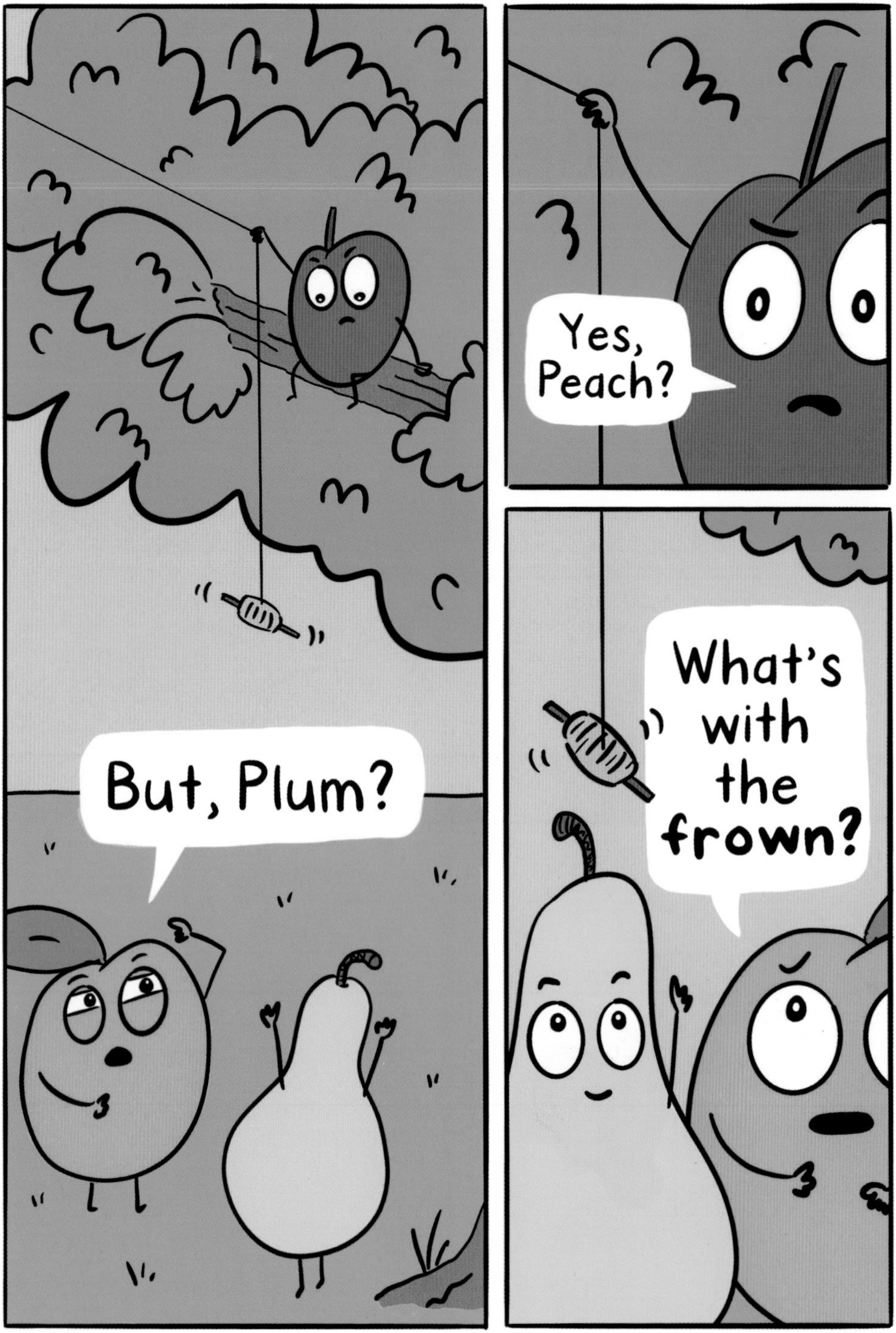
Yes, Peach?
But, Plum?
What's with the frown?

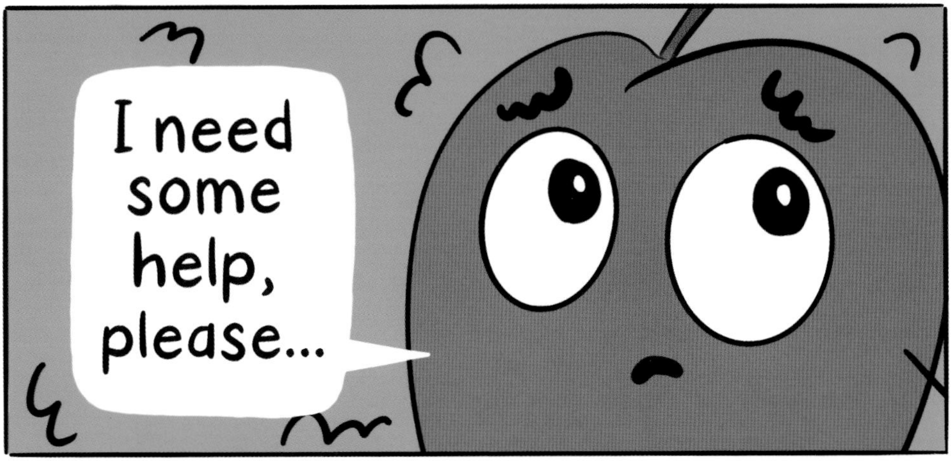
I need some help, please...

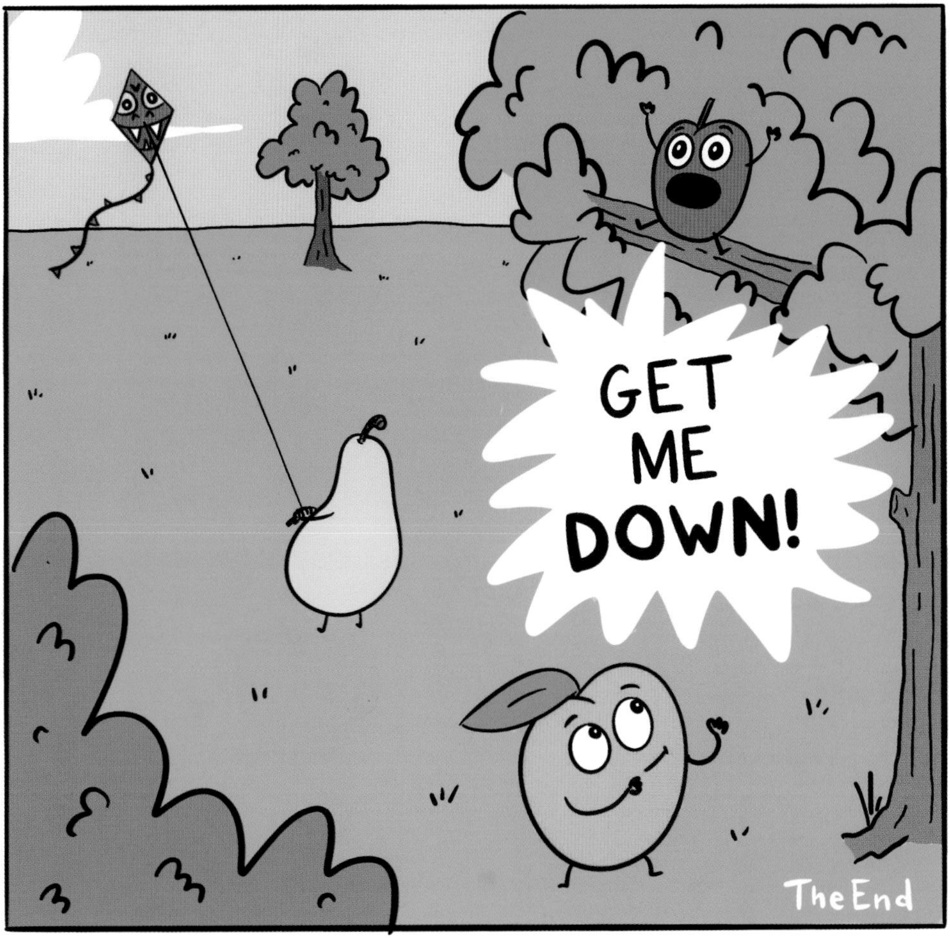
GET ME DOWN!
The End

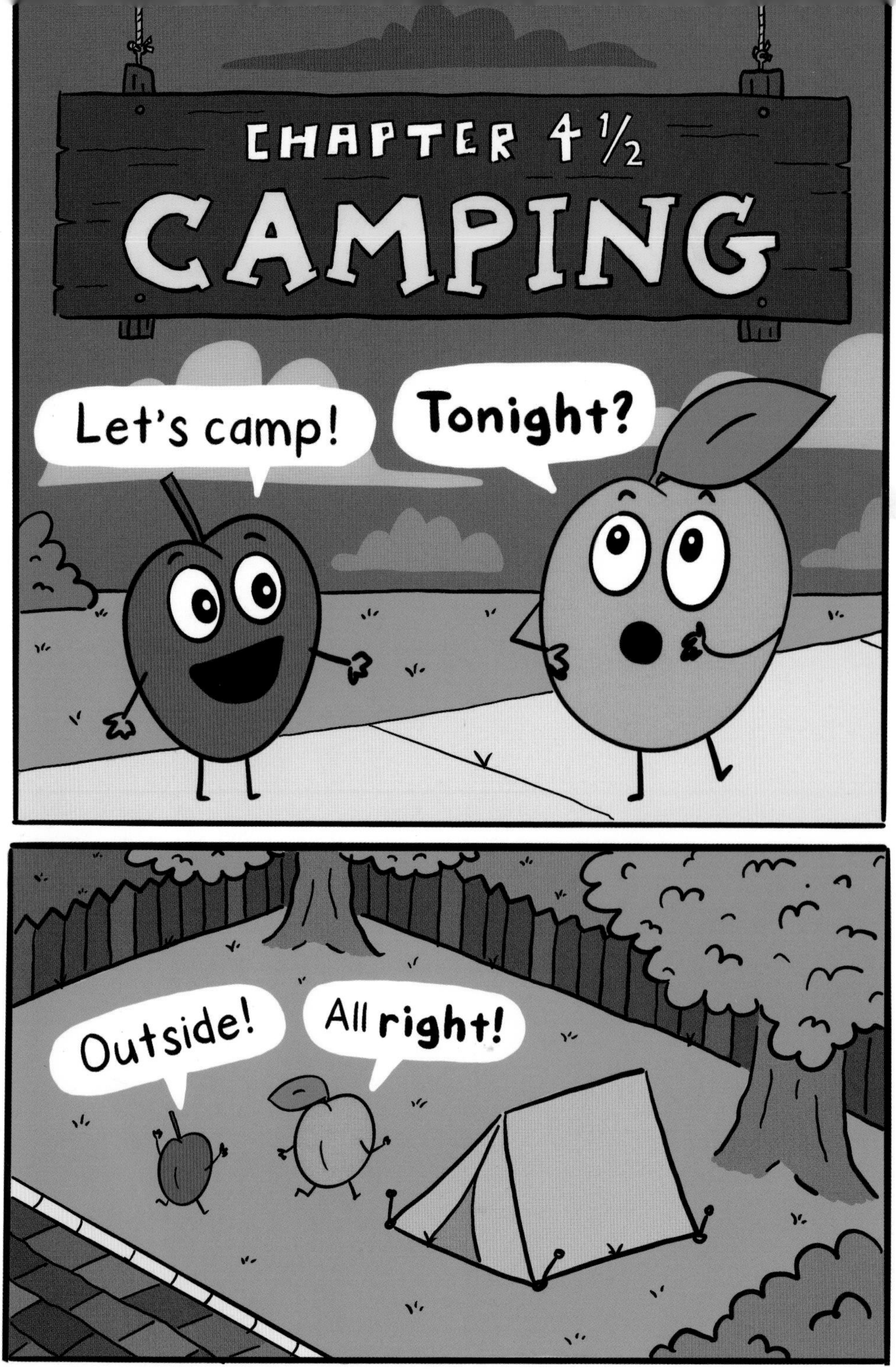
CHAPTER 4 ½
CAMPING
Let's camp!
Tonight?
Outside!
All right!

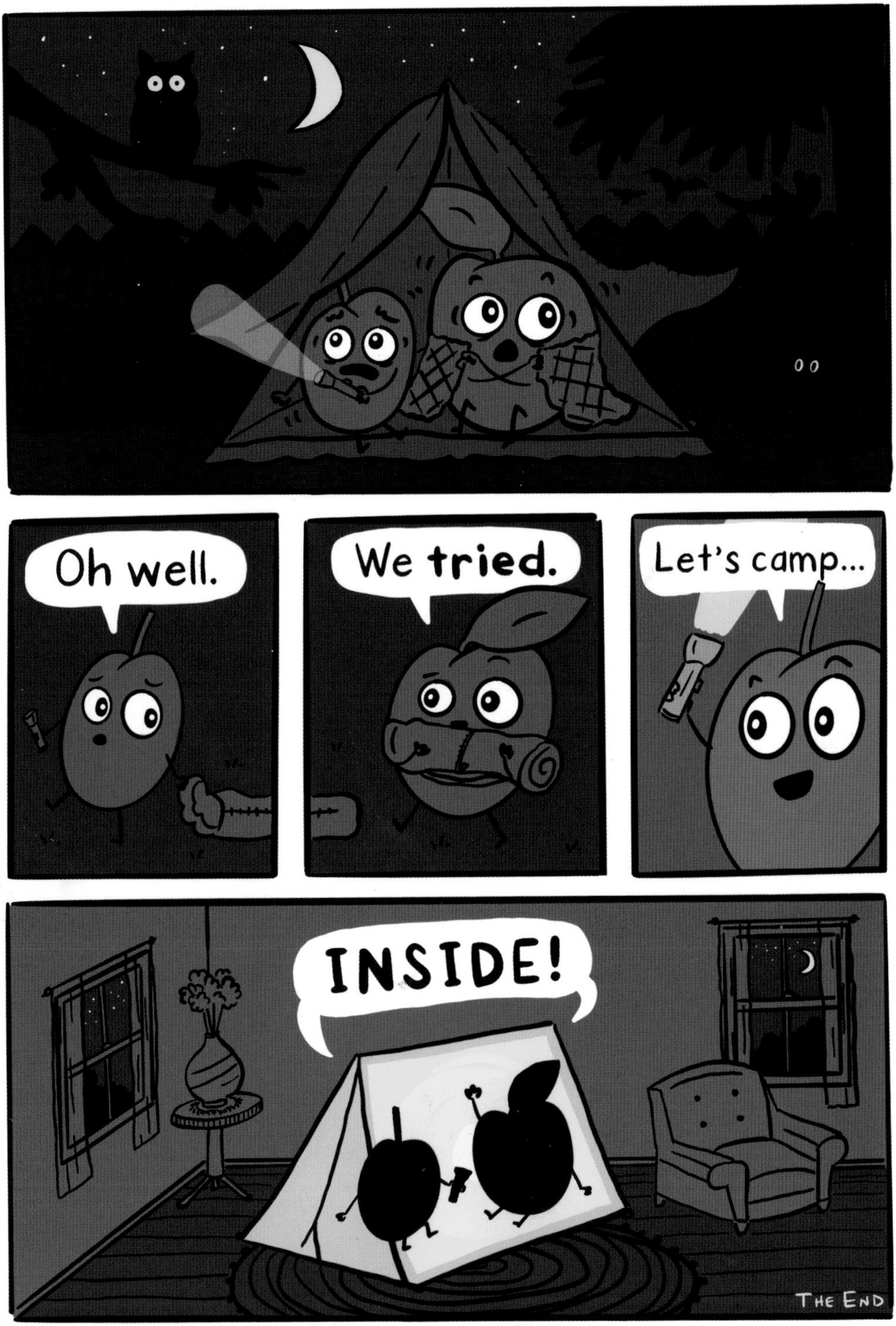

Oh well.
We tried.
Let's camp...
INSIDE!
THE END

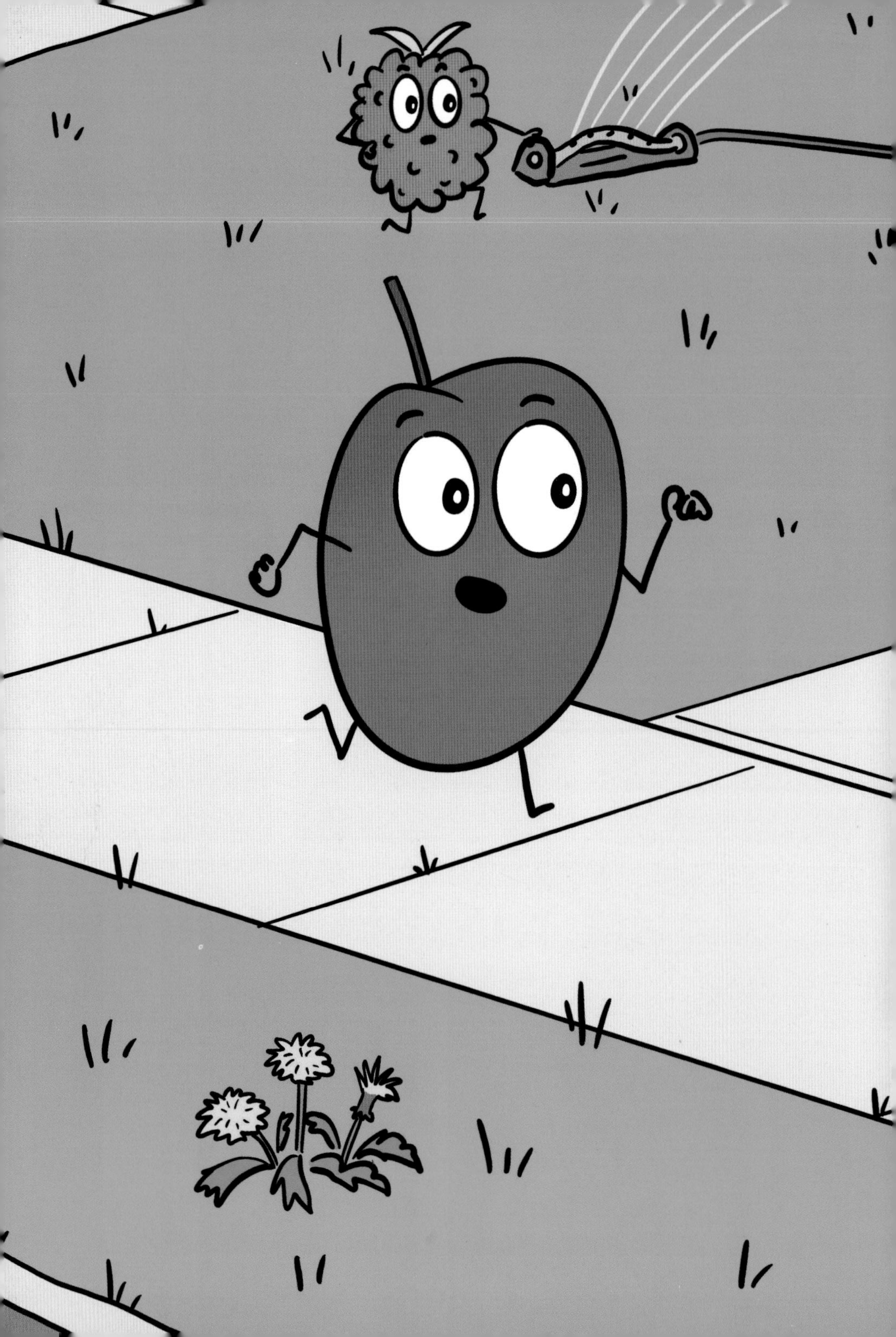

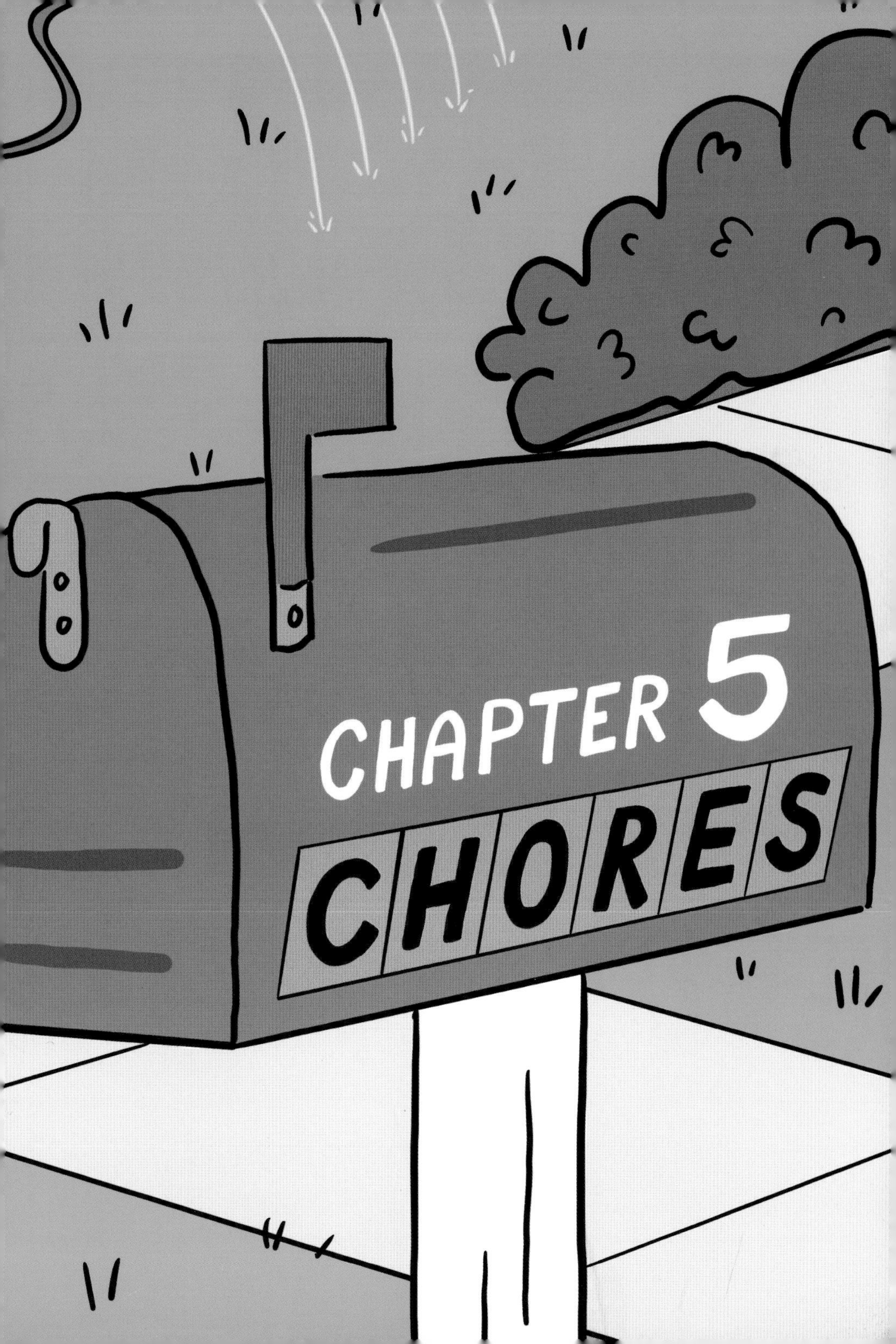
CHAPTER 5
CHORES

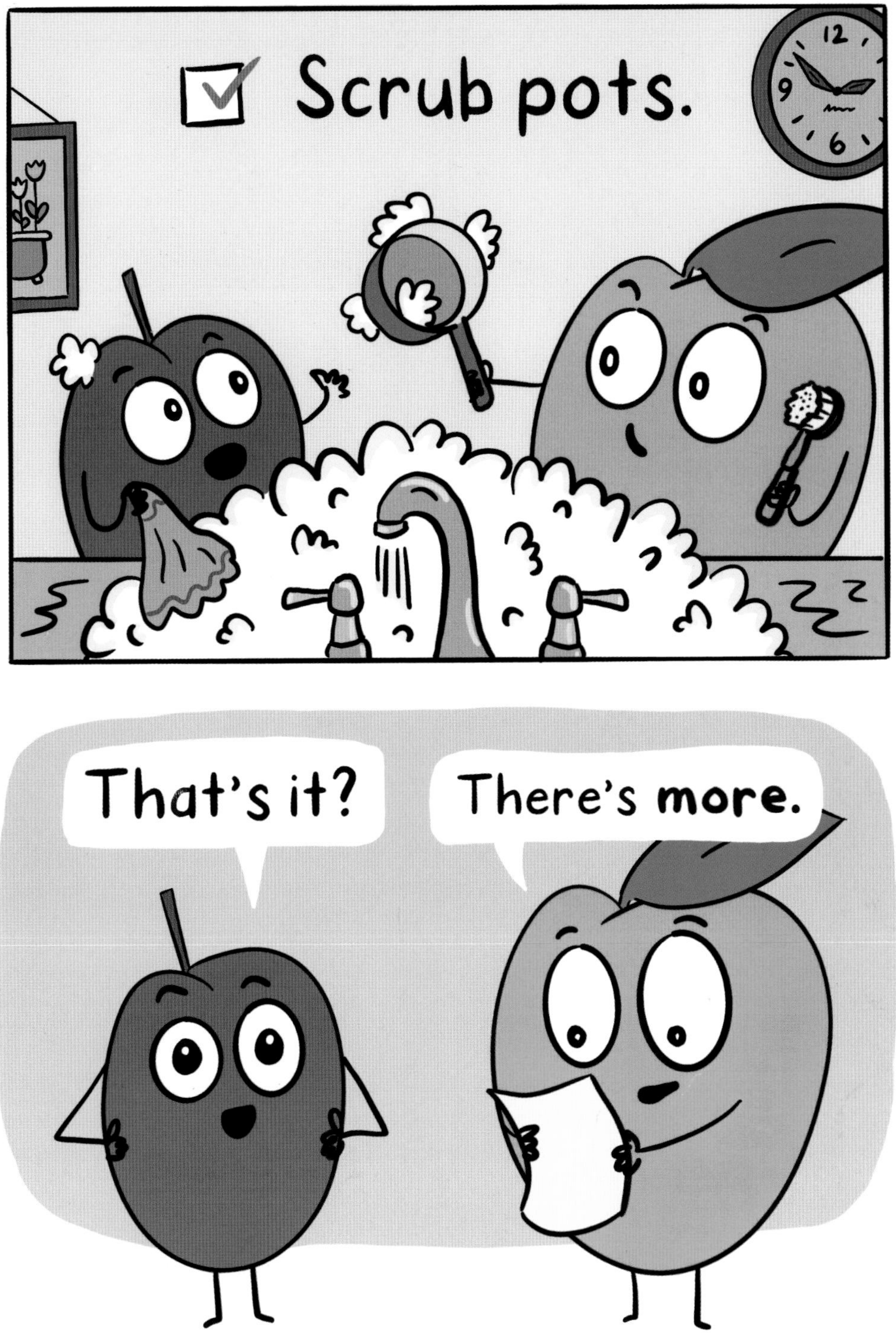

Scrub pots.
12
9
6
That's it?
There's **more.**

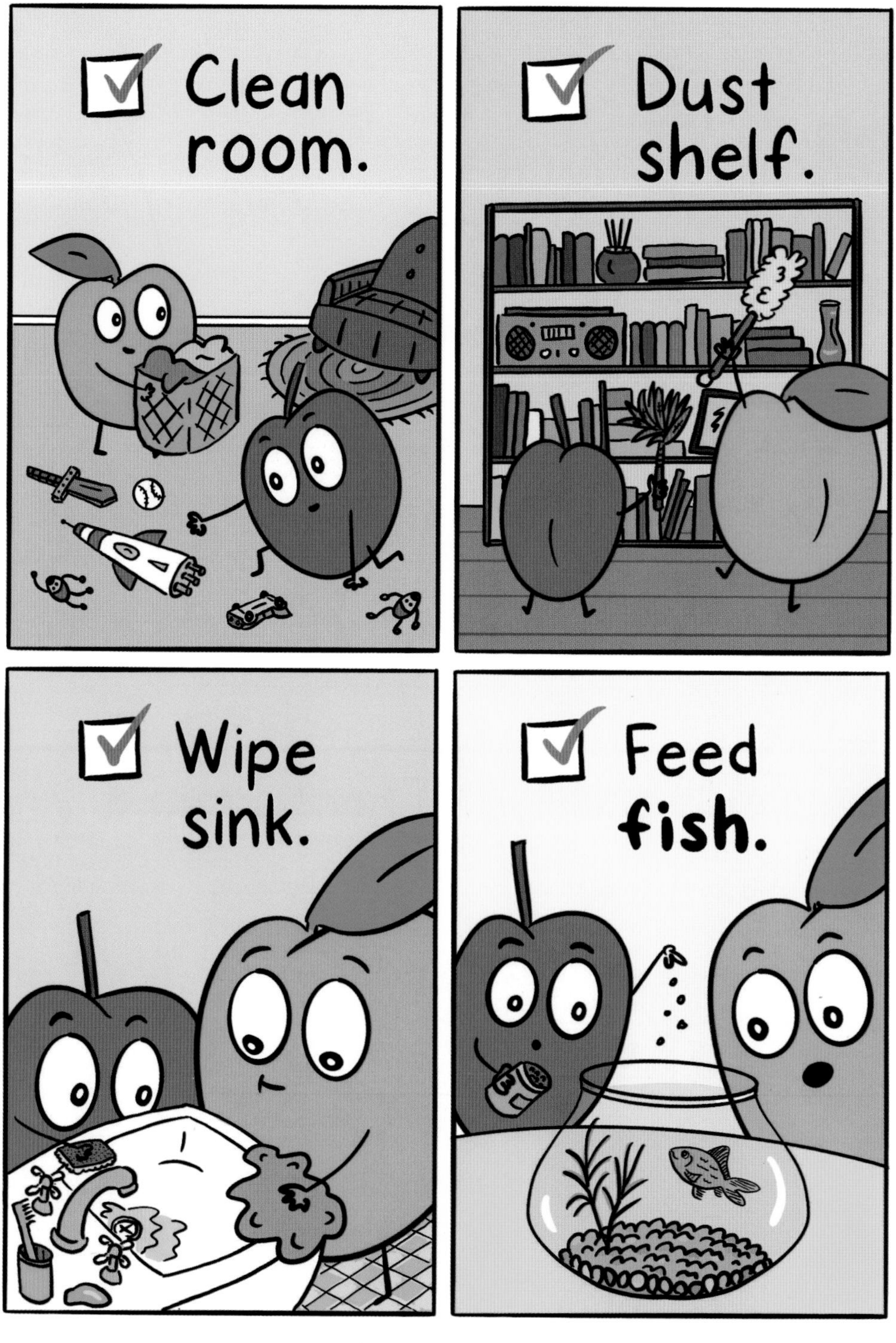
Clean room.
Dust shelf.
Wipe sink.
Feed fish.

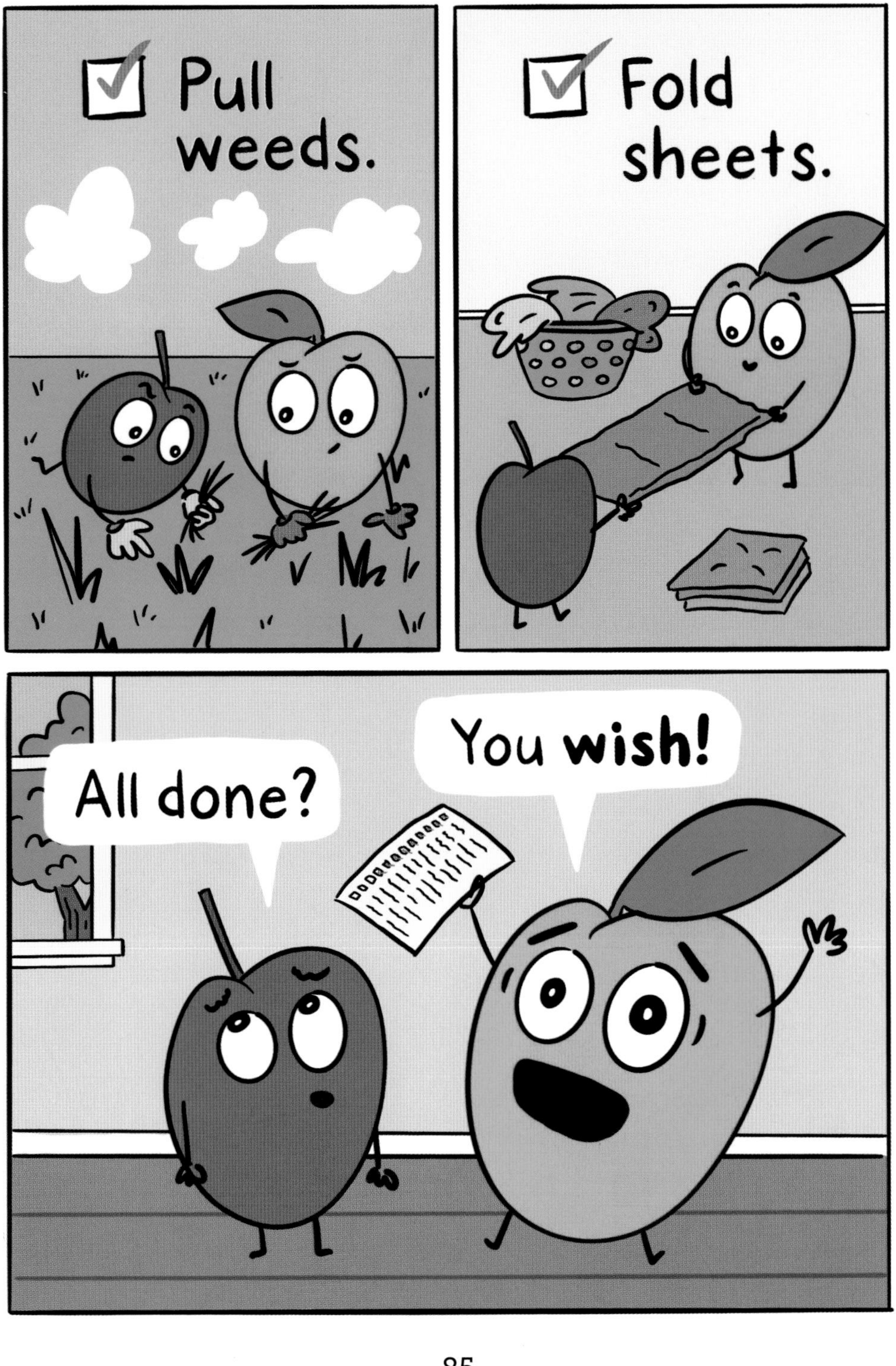
Pull weeds.
Fold sheets.
All done?
You **wish!**

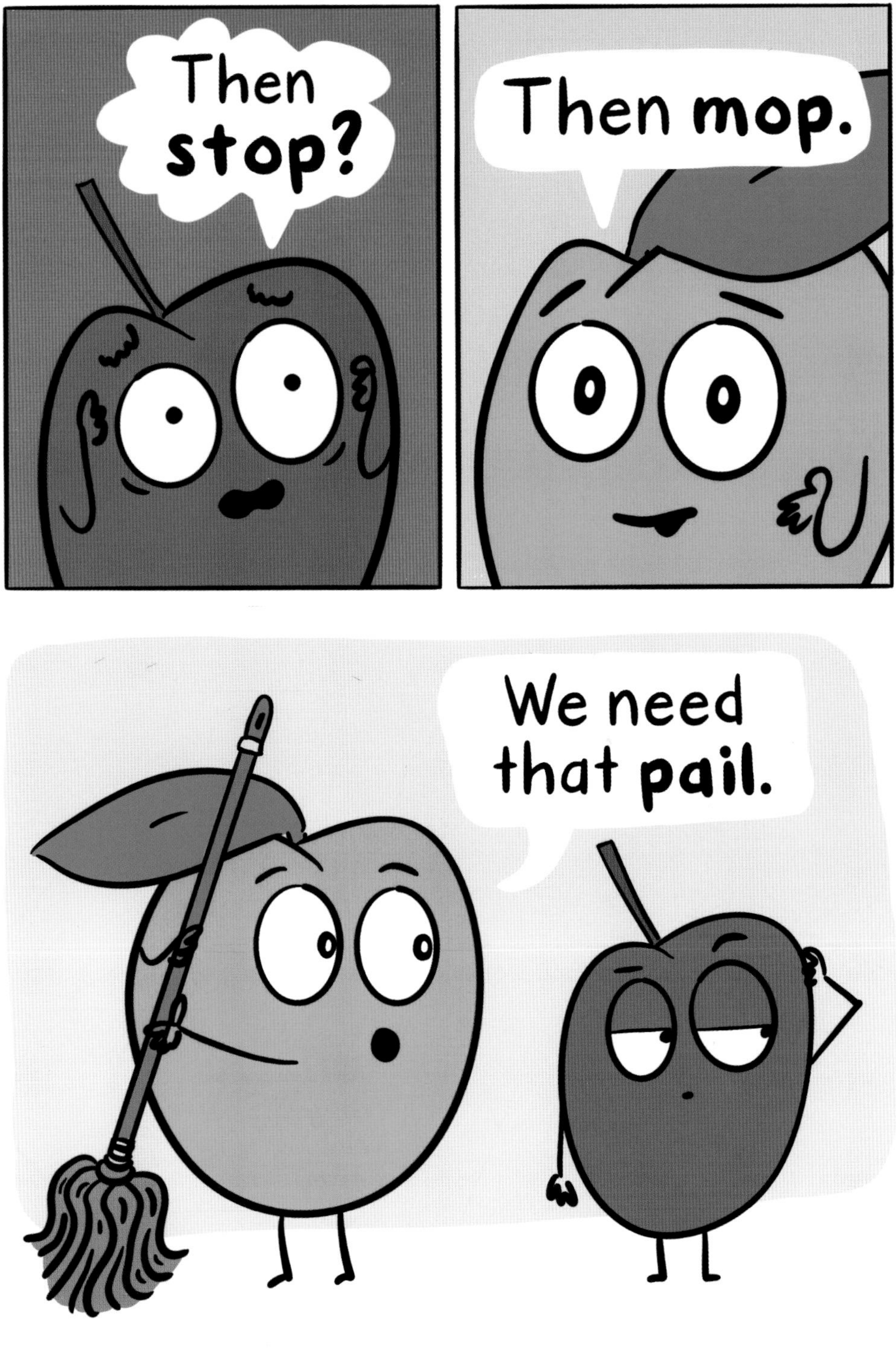
Then stop?
Then mop.
We need that pail.

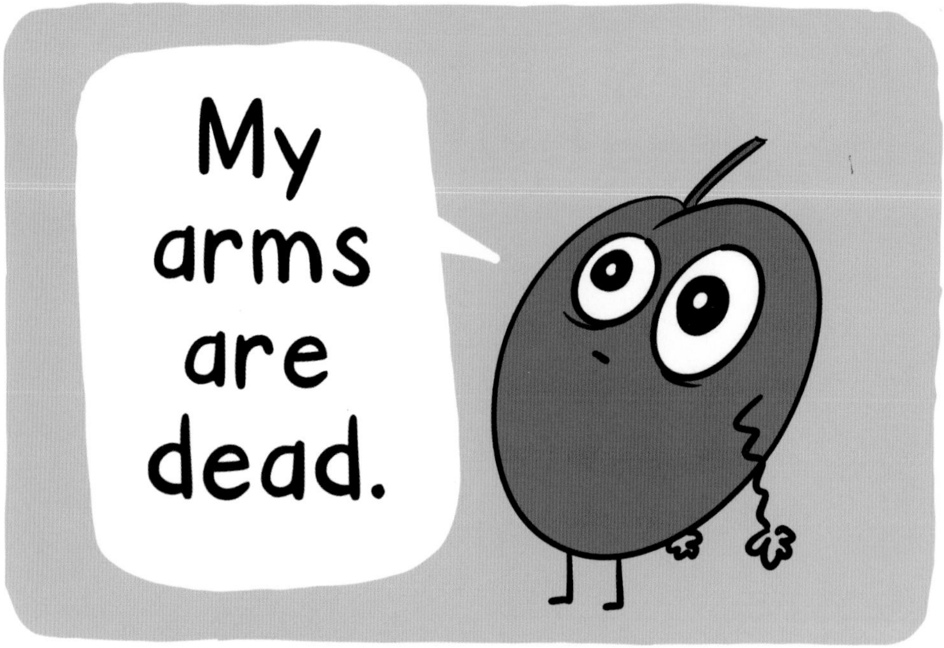
My arms are dead.

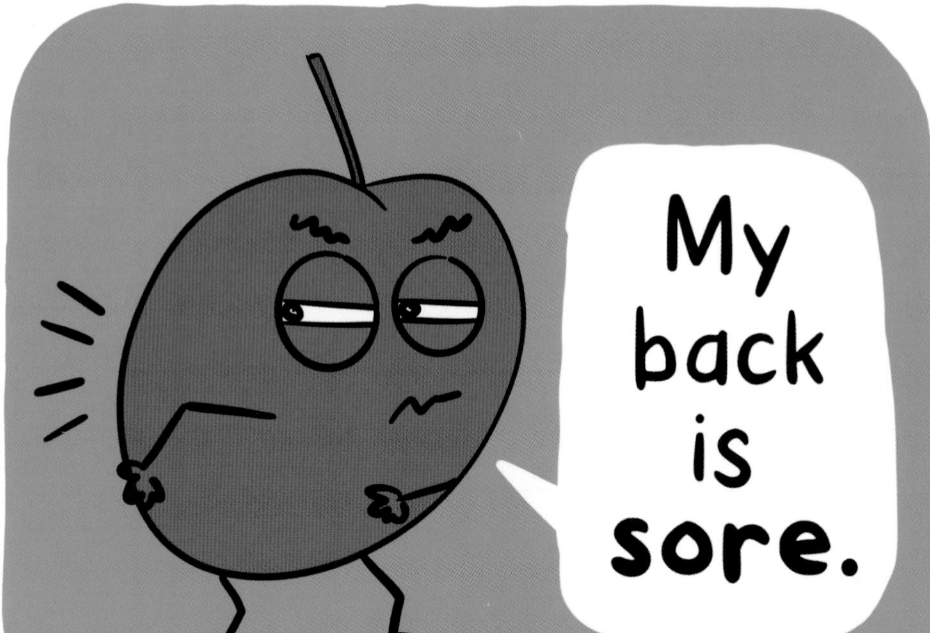
My back is sore.

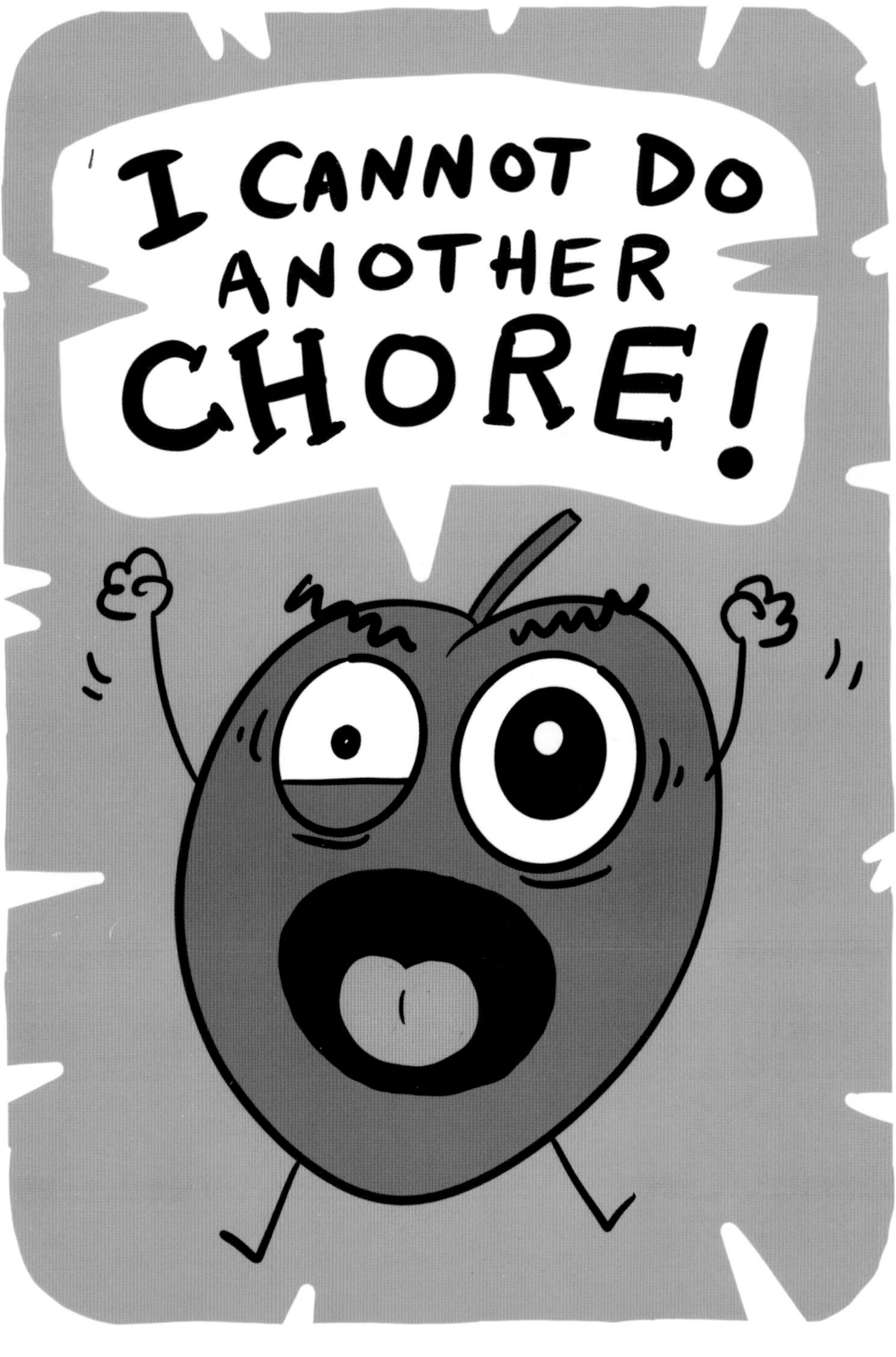
I CANNOT DO ANOTHER CHORE!

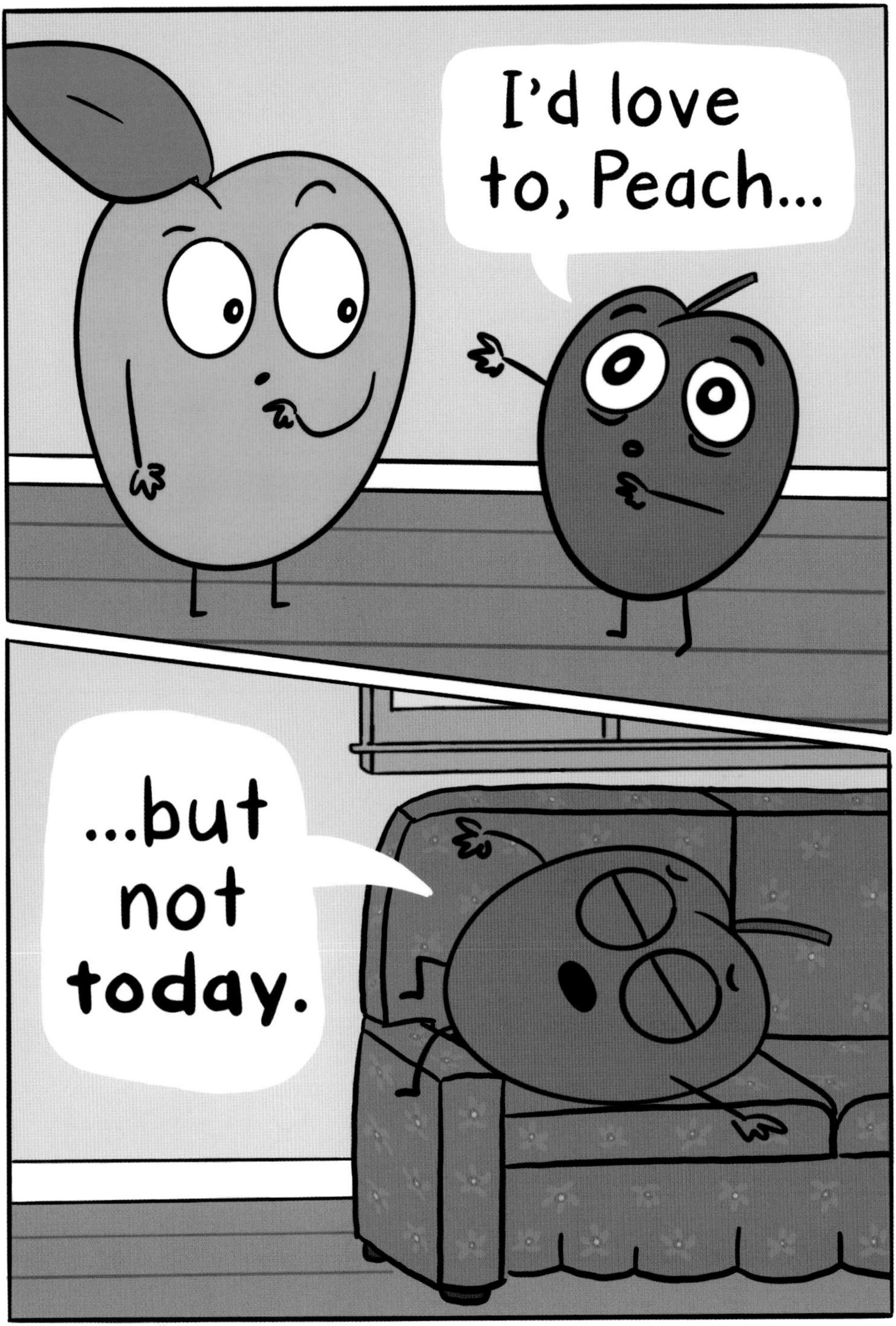
I'd love to, Peach...
...but not today.

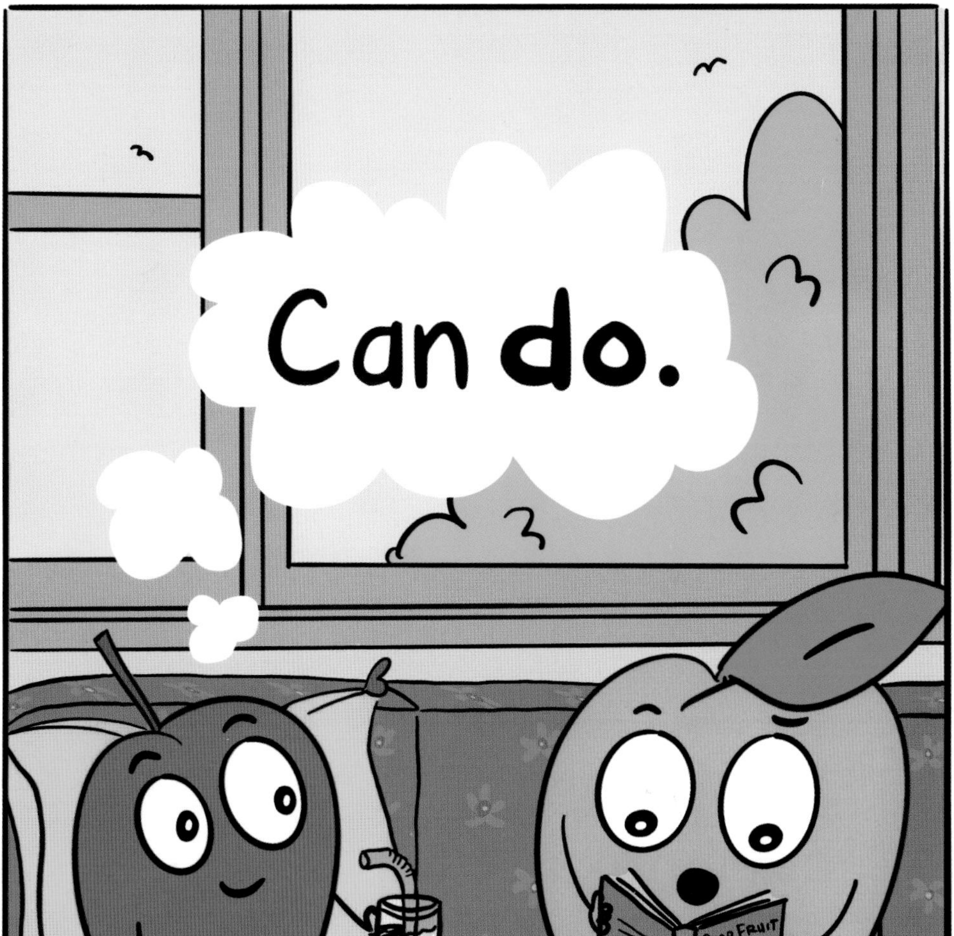
Can do.
STAR FRUIT
THE END

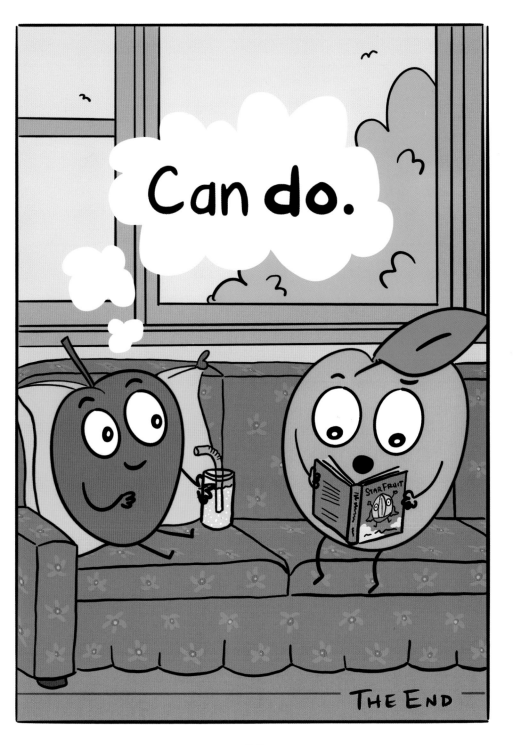

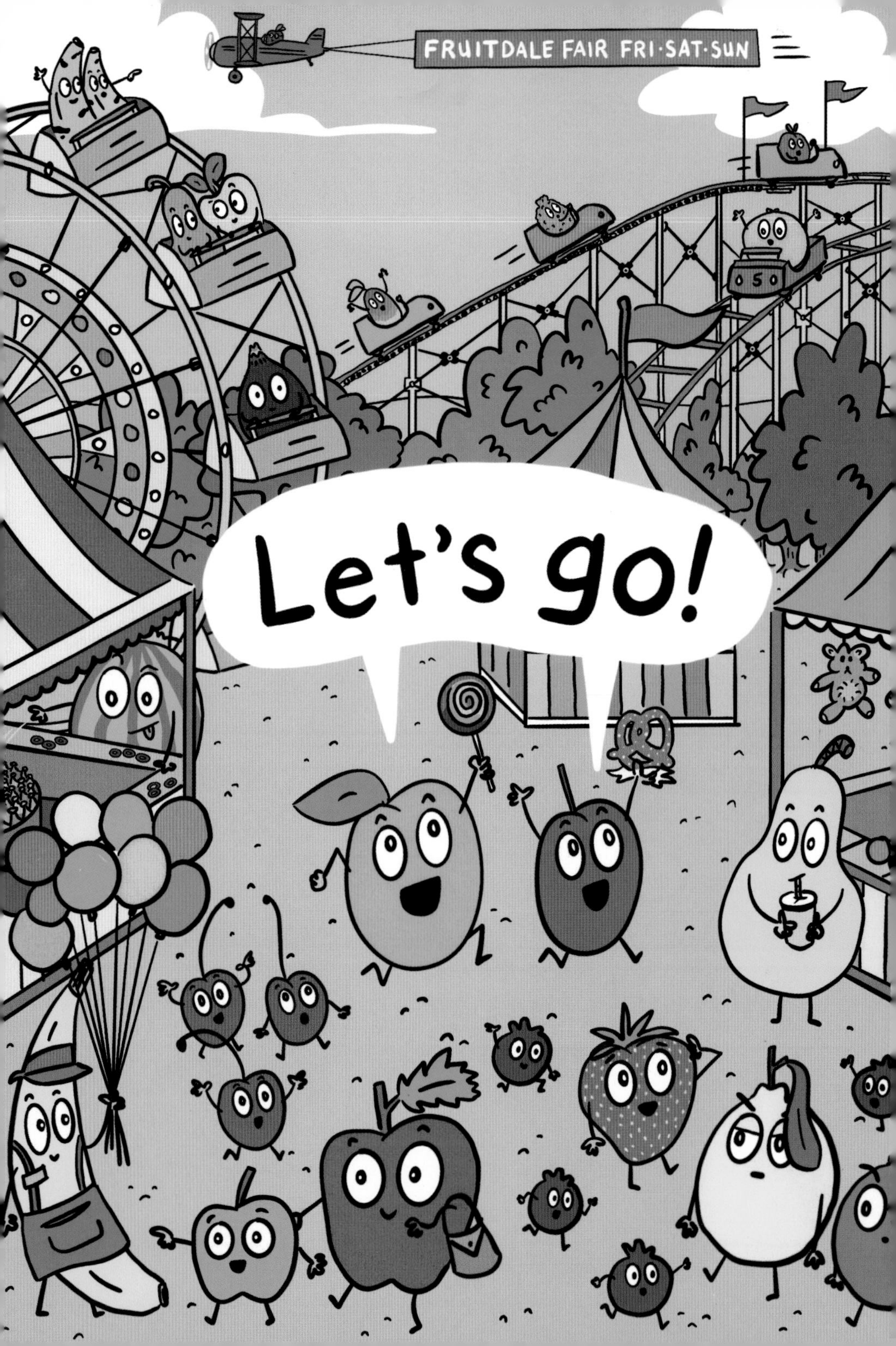
FRUITDALE FAIR FRI·SAT·SUN
50
Let's go!